[Digitare il testo]

Once
Upon
a
Bed
of
Roses

Simon J.
George

Once upon a Bed of Roses...

It's the Spring of 2021, and Francesca Scarpa, a successful Health and Safety Manager of a multinational hotel chain in northern Italy, is about to conclude another taxing week. An accomplished multitasker, she appears to rule the roost over her incompetent male colleagues with consummate ease. Yet in her private life, the strains of managing her pubescent son, Giorgio, and estranged husband, Edoardo, begin to take their toll.

Francesca is forced to wrestle with responsibility and take back control for her colleagues' mistakes. As duty calls, the veneer of her superficial lifestyle begins to peel away, and Chiara - her best friend and confidant – mirrors back Francesca's fickleness, insecurity and loneliness. Intrigue, romance, illness and betrayal all collude to precipitate her midlife crisis. Meanwhile, Edoardo seems to have rekindled the artistic talents of his youth, and his creative juices are in full flow.

Will Francesca dare to look destiny in the eye to find her better self, and can Edo have his cake and eat it? And how will Chiara deal with life-changing events?

Make no mistake, destiny will always give us what we ask for, and more....

*This book is dedicated above all to the memory of Sam,
Lina, Giovanna, Rudi, and Angelo,
all of whom made a hasty departure from this world,
but whose love and affection
I hold in my heart.*

Copyright © Simon J. George 2020

The right of Simon J. George to be identified as the author of this work has been asserted by him in accordance with the Copyright, Designs and Patents Act 1988

Once upon a bed of roses...

How casually words
Fall through my mind,
Latching on to chains of thought
With no discernible connection.

*

And still no order,
As they tumble on an open page
To share a crowded space
With tears of joy and sadness.

*

Let wondrous reverie
Now conspire with life's ordeals
To rise above and fall again
Upon a bed of roses.

***

Part One

The day of reasoning

One

Sitting at the breakfast table, perching, posing, pouting. Up you get Francesca Scarpa, you're not Julia Roberts, and Dick Gere is definitely not going to save you, that's for sure. Today is a stocking day. Yesterday was trouser day, and tomorrow will be skirt day. What about shoes? Well that's still the hardest part, now that I don't do lipstick for work anymore, only gloss. When I was young, lips, belts and shoes were the Bermuda Triangle of fashion for me. I could disappear for hours before I got it all coordinated. Now, it's only shoes that throw me. There they are, dozens of them neatly shelved in the wardrobe, staring at me like broody chickens in a hen coop. These days, I'm more pragmatic - forget colour-coded and style-guided, I'm 100% odour-opted. It's quarter past seven and this morning I have a videoconference with my boss, Mr Conrad at eleven - a debriefing about the cause of the fire in the gourmet restaurant kitchen at the hotel last week. Not looking forward to that. He's a gentleman, rather good taste, but not even would get as far as my shoes. That's way beyond his field of vision - he'll be caught up in my cleavage by five past eleven! It's a man's world and he's no exception to the rule. So what about the shoes?... Minging! Can't wear those. It will have to be the ballerines again. It's the fifth time I've worn them in the past two weeks, but they're not in the wardrobe. So where are they?... In the hall? No…. Under the kitchen table? No….In my sports bag? No… Oh damn! …Ah, here they are. That's right, I left them steaming on the terrace steps a couple of days ago. That's the longest detox they've seen in a while!. If I ever get through this life and reincarnate, I'll be an influencer or a fashion blogger specialising in shoes. Imelda Marcos spent a fortune on shoes. Her husband Ferdinand – I think he was the world's first kleptocrat, - spent more than twenty years amassing a personal fortune that's worth billions. She's outlived him by over thirty years so it's all hers. Now, that's a lot of shoes! She must be ninety. And they certainly were a pioneering family, priding themselves on extravagance, corruption, and brutality – I'm surprised Netflix hasn't done a series on them. Anyway, the Filipinos still haven't learnt their lesson. These days, the antics they got up to are pretty much run-of-the-mill - all the world's presidents are at it: revamp the constitution, silence the press, use violence, oppression and scandal to undermine the opposition, and hold fraudulent referendums, of course. If Britain had studied the history books a little more meticulously, they'd have got Brexit done in a jiffy! And it won't be long before we have martial law in Europe, that's for sure….

But it's such an effort in the mornings with Giorgio. I do everything for him - all the hard graft from breakfast to bedtime: school runs, homework, football training, sleepovers, I even iron his football boot laces, and lord only knows, I'll be managing his love life in a few years' time. At least he's still a boy – he's only twelve and a half - and mum comes first right now. I don't really think he's into girls yet, but he does have a childhood sweetheart....

And then there's Edoardo, my husband. Of course, that makes me his wife and his second mother. Wasn't it a Cosmopolitan survey that said 90% of married Italian men have two mothers ... and the other 10% had three? He's past his prime at fifty-six and definitely regressing. Over breakfast, he slurps his coffee and unashamedly picks inside his nostrils for hard crusties. Yesterday, he even wiped his fortune finger on the tablecloth. And he doesn't even realise he's doing it. Disgusting! ....

At least, I've got the gym to look forward to with Daniele, my personal trainer. Definitely cute with all that bubble butt brawn of his. Oh well, you can't have everything in a man. Last week, with that broad cheesy grin of his, he even asked me out for a sweaty-jock cocktail. That gym bunny is real a fanny teaser. Maria says he's got buns of steel and that I should have my temperature taken with his all beef thermometer... Well hardly! She's the wrong age: forty-eight; and the wrong star sign: Gemini. Everyone knows how promiscuous Gemini's are when they hit their midlife crisis! Anyway, I put all my fantasies in the freezer years ago, and Dick

Wittyless is definitely not pressing my defrost button. I prize brain, power and wealth, but not necessarily in that order, and my legs usually get my men's brains into perspective. Maria got a bit too careless and now she's divorced, single and worst of all, poor....

So, where did I put the car keys? They don't seem to be in my bag.... Got them... But I can't have left them in the medicine cabinet. What was I thinking of? Ah yes, that's right, I had period pains and I went to get a new blister of Brufen, and then Chiara called. Emergency over... Now, let's just check my diary in case I've forgotten anything. Conference call with Conrad at 11:00am, sushi team-building lunch with my team 12:30; manicure 1:30pm; Daniele, gym at 2:30:pm; Angelo, mèche at 5.00, Kundalini-Spinning class at 7.00. Busy day, but I should just about fit it all in.

-"Giorgio, darling, are you ready? What do you mean you've had no breakfast? It's time for school! You'll make me late again for the 5th day in a row! .... No, I can't make it now. You should have been out of bed half an hour ago. No time for a cereal, and I don't give a damn. Get yourself a Kinder Brioss, and brush your teeth, your breath smells."

It's a crazy morning, kids have no respect for mums these days. I should say parents, but in this dystopian entity we call a family, I *am* the parent because Edo is useless. He's an anaesthetist at the city hospital. And he's been in the same job for thirty years, so he's on permanent "low energy" mode now, and his battery isn't recharging. I'm his life support that's for sure. He complains all the time: too many hours, not enough pay, not enough holidays, too many night shifts, and worst of all, occasional night duty at provincial hospitals. When away nights are on his weekly schedule, it's best to stay well out of his way. He never complains about conferences, though. Not that I listen him much. Dinner talk can be utterly distasteful. Last week, he was on nights and his team had to perform an emergency operation on a homeless Nigerian refugee with an acute urethral infection. Can you imagine this guy had gone septic at the base of his penis. I say the base, because that's all he had, according to Edo. The rest of his attributes had been mutilated in a tribal feud. That's why he was granted refugee status apparently. All the same, penile persecution and purulent urethral discharge definitely don't titillate my taste buds!

-"Giorgio darling, two minutes, okay?"

I make so many sacrifices for him. But he's my bright star. I am his willing slave mother. And I should be proud of that! After all, Giorgino plays on the best cadet football team in town and goes to the exclusive private school. And I pay for all of it. My husband doesn't contribute to my son's education. I don't want that. To his credit, he pays the mortgage, so he does come in handy for something, after all....

It's 7.30am and time to scramble. It's only a five minute walk to Giorgio's school, but with a 50K company car, a BMW sports cabrio, who'd want to walk? I don't care anything about cars other than their colour, but I do get a kick out of seeing the other mums' heads turn when we arrive. So, for this car I chose *Traumschwarz* – dream black. It reminds me of my German *aupair*, Isotte, who was so warm and friendly in stark contrast to my fake 'Teutonic' mother, who was an honorary member of the *Schutzstaffel*.

-"Giorgio, move it, or you'll be marching to school!"

***

Two

-"Oh my God, look at the damn traffic, bumper to bumper, and we're not getting anywhere. Christ! Did you see that Giorgino? He just cut me off and shoved his fat-arsed Mercedes Four Wheel Drive right in front of me. You utter twat!.... So Giorgio, today is Friday, and in my book that makes it our meaningful chat morning while I run you to school. What have you got to tell me about your week, honeykin?
-Don't call me that, mama, you know I hate it. What's a twat, anyway?
-It's a twit with and "A" sound!

-And why are you always so stroppy? We read at school that more than 81% of our mums are stressed out by their kids.

-What? That's nonsense, and you know how much I love you. Listen, career mums have a lot on their plates, especially when their husbands - and by that I mean your biological father in particular – don't lift a finger around the house or contribute to the ménage. And anyway, even if he did, that would mean more than double the work for me. But do you really think I'm stressed Giorgio? You know you are such a wonderful super sensitive kid, with really advanced social skills for a 12 year old; you're just streets ahead of the others. You could be an actor you know. But back to our meaningful conversation about you, so put your Playstation back in your backpack. You know that's forbidden in the car. It's bad for your eyes.

-Mama, what's it like to be gay, you know, homosexual? Dad calls it perverted, and says that I'd better not turn out like that or he'll take me off the football team.

-Oh, there he goes again, your dad's a genius. He wants you to grow up to be a homophobe.

-What's that?

-A gay hater! Anyway, he can't stop you playing football because it's me that decides everything about that. I pay for your club membership. And you can tell him that the next time he has one of his rants and raves.

-Jesus Christ! You prick! Did you see that Giorgio?... The fucking shit-brained cocksucker. He just turned left without even indicating. I nearly drove right up his

jacksie. Typical! That dick-head in the Merc has got no fucking road sense. He's only got that car for status! ...
-Mama!
Sorry Giorgio, you're right. I get so wound up by male chauvinist pigs! Anyway, on the subject of gays, most of them are really nice people; I have several gay friends, and they're creative, smart and most of them have great dress sense. My hairdresser, Angelo, is gay and look what a wonderful job he does with my highlights. He's so artistic, my colour is unique. You'd never know I have grey roots, would you? They are really sensitive and great company too, and gays give great advice to mums on how to manage their numbskull husbands. But you must be careful with them, because they bitch about other people like there's no tomorrow.
-But what does it mean when people say they're homosexual mum? Tom says they put their dicks up other men's bums and have lots of sex".
-Look Giorgio that's not funny, ok? I don't allow you to say "dick" in my company, so I don't want to ever hear you saying say those things, or anything similar again. It's okay to say that gay men love other men, not women, and that's the women's fault anyway... and some of them are even married today, because gay people have feelings and that's why they have the same rights as we do. So no more "willy" conversations, thank you. That's your dad's department. One day, you will understand that feeling each other and feeling for each other are just about mutually exclusive.

- Well, you called that man in the Mercedes a cocksucker! And Thomas says that gays cook socks, and that women do too, 'cos he's seen them doing it on movies. Mum do you cook socks?

-Jesus, spare my weeping soul. If I ever hear you say another word about this, I'll knock that head of yours right off its block. Never mind washing your mouth out with soap. You have a vile mouth, and you should be ashamed of yourself! I'm going to have words with Tom's mum about this. Now get out of the car. You're late for school and you've gone and made me late too.

-Mum, what did I say wrong? You never listen to me. I said 'cooking socks', honest. …Mama, who's picking me up from football practice today, anyway?

-What's that? Football? I completely forgot. At 6:30pm as usual?

-Mama, don't be late again."

Nightmare - I'm going to have to rearrange my whole afternoon. I'll phone Angelo to see if I can bring forward the mèche, otherwise I'll be late for Giorgio again and we didn't exactly get off to a good start today, so it's probably going to be a toss-up between nails and the gym. Gemma or Daniele? Well they can wait. Obviously, I wasn't' going to do Kundalini –bike on a mèche day. I always double book with Kundalini-bike, just in case I'm having a major crisis. It's a great way to combine physical exertion and meditative contemplation. It really balances me, and after a week like this, I ought to go… I'd better call anyway, but I can't tell her I'm skipping because of

Giorgio's football training, otherwise I'll get a half-hour sermon on female slavery in the 21st century! Thank God, I've got my new iPhone 11 with its A13 bionic chip, otherwise I wouldn't have a life except for everything that's going on in my mind. My head is an unchartered jungle.

***

Three

-"Tristan, is that you? Yes it's me Francesca. I was just about to call you… What, you want to cancel because Angela needs a wig fitting? Come on Tristan, it's my roots and mèche day. I can't miss that. The grey is showing through. I've been doing my Iris Apfel impersonation with these thick black-framed glasses all week as a decoy, but three of my female colleagues got themselves into a frenzy about it. Actually, I wanted to suggest coming earlier…. What if I come at 4.30? ….Well, I suppose I could do, but that means missing my gym session with my personal trainer…. Yes you're right hair is important… and I know she lost all her hair last week… Listen, that's okay for me. Poor Angie!"

Friday is always a hassle for hair. I'm not giving up my spot for anyone, not even for Angela. It is so awful that her chemo cycle is making her hair fall out. But my hair is my pride and joy and it's always been like that since the days mum called me Goldilocks, and that's how it's always going to be. That was the only affectionate thing she ever said to me as a child. And that's why it means so much to me. Look at Goldie Hawn, she's still blond and she'll be a fossil in 10 years, so why can't I be blond and stay blond? Especially as tomorrow I have to get my new outfit for the annual conference. This year it's in Rome, and I've been dieting for it for 6 weeks!

-"Sanjeet Kaur, it's Franci. Listen, can I call you Wanda today? I'm having a crazy day and I can't be doing with your Sai Baba snack name.
-*Sat Nam*, Francesca, peace be with you. You know that's my Sikh name. Sanjeet means victorious and Kaur is the surname given to Sikh women by the 10th Sikh guru, Guru Gobind Singh. It means "princess" and it was given to Sikh women as a symbol of equality between women and men, and that's why my mission is to be the Princess of devotion to equality and sexual healing between women and men."
-Whatever…
-Well, what can I do for you, my dear martyred Francesca?
-Look Wanda, I'm terribly groggy today. I've had a headache for days and my stomach's in knots again. I've definitely got period pains and maybe I'm menopausal. There's just no way I can do the class tonight. I'm so distraught, believe me, and my roots are showing grey again. You know me, I wouldn't miss the lesson for anything, but..

-You've booked in at the hairdressers, right? Weren't you going to change to Thursdays? I'll send you the menopause *Kriya*. It's a meditation you have to day everyday for 20 days; it's only twenty-one minutes and it will give you vigour and energize your vulva, to prevent the onset of menopause for at least three years. I've been doing it regularly for the past fifteen years and I'm still not menopausal and I'm 62 next month.

-Wanda that's amazing! Are you serious? Thanks a trillion. You're so understanding and balanced and kind-hearted.

-I'm dead serious. Mind over body – that's my motto! It's comes at a cost, but it's a shame you can't come, though. Today's kundalini-spinning class is dedicated to a new journey. I've put together a special compilation of Himalayan rippling streams and Laotian flute music to accompany us on our metaphysical ascent of Everest. I've had to extend the class by 15 minutes. This is a tough one. Anyway, we'll be repeating it on Monday evening, so you don't have to miss out. And don't forget our annual trip to Assisi? Saint Francis is going to cleanse our souls again. By the way, I know you've paid your annual subscription, but how are we doing with the classes? Here, it says you haven't paid for any lessons this year and we're already nearing the end of March.

-Yes, you're right, next week, next week. You know I'm always forking out for Giorgio. Last week new football boots and now he needs a new pair of *Nike Revolution* trainers. He'll only wear Nike and none of the kids at school will wear black trainers now, so he wants fluor.

Can you believe it? I only got him the black pair at Christmas. ...Oh, Oh, Wanda, it's my boss calling me on my other mobile. Catch up soon... *Wahe guru!*"

Now that's what I call a great exit strategy. Can't believe that woman. She's so tight when it comes to money, and no compassion for working mothers, either. At least a discount. And all that twinkle-toe trash about being the princess of equality and sexual healing. She's a praying mantis. Any hetero guy that comes along to kundalini-spinning is after a quick shag, everyone knows that; either that, or they're deluded gay mystics. Either way, sex is never far from the top of their agendas. And most of the heteros stuff socks down their jocks to bulge better, and she falls for it every time. I'll never forget Angus beefing up the revs so much that he didn't notice his wife's *Noémie Lenoir* stocking dangling out of his pants until it got tangled in the sprocket. That certainly catapulted him into a new dimension, and when he crunch-landed on the head stem it was excruciating. Gemma said it was a crash course in transexuality By the time Irene croaked up that it put a whole new perspective giving head, I'd just lost it. Not so gifted after all, Angus Ball-Breaker! Well, Wanda's great on equality and all that, but when it comes to the sexual healing, she's like a *Kinder Surprise*. Everyone is dying to get to crack the egg open, but once you take off the wrapping, nobody wants the surprise! Fleeting joys indeed. Well, perhaps that's a bit mean to think of Wanda like that. She's been a tower of strength for me, especially after my miscarriage. And she's had a hard time getting to be a princess. Her husband was an alcoholic and prone to beating her and it took a haemorrhaged spleen to get her out of that home. She's another one of triple H-ers (from home, to hospital, to hostel) and I've seen it happen so many times. She must be lonely. Ten years up on Nirvana before nose-diving into Angus's jocks….poor thing! That Kriya does sound interesting though. I wonder if it will stop my premature greying roots too…

***

Four

Is that the time already? Almost eleven o'clock and I haven't had breakfast. Last night was a tough one. Delivering twins at 3.30am, and what with all the complications. It just took forever to get the epidural catheter placement right for the caesarean birth. The Filipino women are so petite. How on earth do they do twins? But God made us, I suppose, and that includes the monozygotic too...Well that should keep the national statistics office happy. But after a night like that, even breakfast will be trial and tribulation.. Oops, I've slopped my coffee on the floor again; and the milk pan boiled over again – that's more dried milk stains on the hob. If I was at work, the nurses would clean that up. I'll have to talk to Franci about getting a microwave again. But she's such hard work, once she gets it into her head that it's bad for you..Just like my mother in that sense - strange, how similar they are. Oh shit, now I've gone and dropped sugar spoon again, so that's sticky sugar crystals all over the kitchen surface.. I've always got such bad coordination after night shift... Never mind, Franci will clean it up. She did say to put the dirty dishes in the sink because I'm incapable of loading the dishwasher – I've got no sense of economy of space, she said. I can hear her dulcet tones ringing through the kitchen now!... There we go, at least that's sorted. So what about the half-eaten banana? That can go back in the fruit bowl; and the jammy toast crusts and the half-hearted attempt at a chocolate mousse? Better just leave those here on the side by the hob; I've never been much good at waste separation. Right, let's see what's on TV.

...I'm not watching that propagandistic shit they call news, and I hate cooking programmes. TV is just hooking up the masses. When I was a student, we had ideals. I was a communist, a PLO supporter - I've still got my Yasser Arafat headscarf to show for it - and I'm proud to say, a great fucker - if I wasn't too drunk. But at least I never did drugs. So many of us got wasted on weed, and not just that. How did the saying go? "A whiff of muff will make me stiff?" Or was it "a puff"? Well, something like that... Can't remember now. But that student let in the town centre...we had no idea there was floozy on the top floor. It didn't take us long to find out though. Lip service from the cunning linguists was twenty thousand lire, and friggin' in the riggin, fifty. And that poor Virgin Mary statue... we kidnapped her from the *God Squaddies'* flat downstairs; we put her halo through her praying hands and transformed her into the most pious toilet paper holder in Christendom. And we always used to have laugh about the fact the Tiziano Vecellio was on a 50,000 lire note. "Just off to paint the penitent Mary Magdalene", we'd say. Well, Tiziano lived to the ripe old age of 104. He had a pretty turbulent sex life too, and it was rumoured that he got more than a sticky paintbrush while he was daubing his oils on Roman goddesses. Today, education has become a seductive affair for big business – paying for good grades and running up debts everywhere, and then our politicians have got the nerve to complain about brain drain. Welcome to the global economy where we put profits before people, and we never hesitated for one second before relocating all our industries to Asia for cheap labour. Now, we've got to foot the bill for that too, while the bastard entrepreneurs pocket the profits. At least in our days, getting drained for every last droplet didn't require brains! We were just fumbling and bungling our way into manhood - irresponsible and without any guidance. It wasn't that easy staying sane, believe me. Life is a bit of a lottery.

I am fifty-six now and almost too old to care about a sex life. You know, I haven't had a sniff, whiff, or been stiff with Franci for over a decade. She just about switched off after Giorgio was born and she's been in lockdown ever since. We did have a good time in the beginning, and that lasted for a couple of years or so. We went out a lot and travelled at weekends, and we didn't care about money;

we've always had enough of that. Then I got my promotion and we moved here for my job. I bought a big apartment not too far from the hospital and we moved in together… At forty-two I made my first major commitment when I took out the mortgage on the flat; at forty-three, my second, when Franci and I got married, and I was forty-four when Giorgio was born. I'm never going to get a medal for bravery for having done any of those things, am I? I've never been the adventurous type. After Francesca had Giorgio, she wanted to get straight back into her career. That's about it I suppose, especially after Franci lost our second child. Couples just get bored of each other's company. It must be all that repetition. Now we do the occasional dinner party, and the rounds with the grandparents. How I hate routine! I need space, freedom, my time. She's got Giorgio and she spoils him awfully. That's what keeps Franci going. She's oblivious to me. I guess it's all about the survival of the fittest. And my middle-aged spread is definitely not helping me out in that department. But I could always try getting a helping hand, I suppose. My colleague, Renato, said that tinder gave him a second lease of life, but I've never been on a chat before. All my colleagues are at it. I'm on afternoons today….. Oh Christ, the toilet roll's run out again. Now, I'm going to have to straggle across the bathroom to the closet in the hope that Bolsonaro's left me a gift from the rainforests.

***

Five

-"*Traumsssschwaaaarz*!
-Yes, darling? You're yelling at me! I'm about to start a conference call with my Director. Call me after eleven-thirty."
-There's no bleeeeeeding toilet paper in the bathroom!
-Wet wipes. My chest of drawers, second drawer down, left-hand side. Always there in an emergency. Speak later!"

He hasn't got a clue. He's the baby that never grew up, and I spend my life cleaning up after him. God only knows what I'll find tonight. Here's Conrad on Skype.

-"Morning Mr. Conrad.
-Morning Francesca. We've got a lot of things to go through here, and I've got a briefing with the board about the fire incident after lunch. So let's clear up this maintenance mystery. The Gandalf Group has just made it into the top ten on the Gold List for destination hotels in Europe, and this year we're competing for the global recognition. It's too serious to joke about, and if the press get wind of it, we could be in for a hammering. So can you give me an update?
-Well, … as I said yesterday, we can't have another fire incident like this, with a meltdown in the kitchen because the cleaner left a four litre container of *Chante Clair* degreaser fluid on the hob, and accidentally switched the deep fryer on while scrubbing it down. We had chemical

warfare in there and it could have gone nuclear. That night, security staff acted swiftly and were at the scene of the fire within minutes of it breaking out. But we've got to strengthen procedures. They are crucial in a company like ours. If we don't have the correct procedures in place, we can't manage an emergency. It's as simple as that. You can't foresee everything, I mean like human error, but you can come pretty close, so that's why we have to overhaul our global cleaning standards and procedures for our kitchens. After the break-in at the storehouse last year, I introduced the Electronic Sign-Off Procedure, ESOP, which is now being deployed globally, requiring security staff to sign off for CCTV surveillance every fifteen minutes.

-But why didn't the water sprinklers activate?

-Of course, there was the issue of the water sprinklers not activating, as you know. This is a problem that has to be clarified with the Maintenance Department. I'm definitely not responsible for that, so you need to speak with Stewart Mutton there. In any case, the fire service arrived in less than ten minutes, and thanks to their prompt action, they were able to contain the fire and prevent it spreading to the restaurant or adjacent buildings. We had one casualty, a security guard who was the first to reach the scene of the incident. He was caught by the small explosion and is in hospital with mostly minor burns. He's stable, and should be home in 10 days.

-Well thank you for that Francesca. That seems quite clear. But I still don't understand why the water sprinklers didn't activate.

-As I said, Mutton is responsible for that. I had specifically asked to be updated on maintenance conformity documentation four times this year, which is all confirmed by emails, but he has never replied to them, so I really can't give you any more information than that at present. Our procedures are a complete mess, Mr. Conrad. We really need to look at roles and responsibilities in top management too.

-What was the condition of the hob prior to the fire?

-The same applies to maintenance certification for all the kitchen equipment. I'm waiting for an update from Mutton.

-The loss damage consultant is coming to make an assessment on Monday morning at 10.00, right? Once he's been, we can start work on repairs. Francesca, our focus needs to be on reopening as soon as possible. The *Matka* gourmet restaurant must be operative for the Easter Bank Holiday weekend. And that's in two weeks.

-Francesca, can you be more specific about the injuries suffered by your security staff member?

-Yes, the security guard is stable, and he's under observation. The explosion happened as he was opening the fire door, so the door took the brunt of the impact. Most of his burns are superficial, partial thickness burns - second degree - to the left side of his scalp, but some are deep partial - third degree – to and around his left ear. He'll probably need some plastic surgery, but it's too early to say at the moment. He should be out of hospital in 10 days. The CCTV revealed that he was actually smoking as he approached the kitchen fire safety door from the outside. So, it's not clear whether he contributed to - or was the cause of the explosion - at the moment. That's being dealt with by the fire service.

-Are you saying he flouted your procedures?

-Well yes, he did.... Of course he had done a training course two years ago, and that is normally repeated every twelve months. Last December's annual fire prevention course was dropped due to budget cuts from head office. And we have to follow orders. That was officially justified as part of the cost-saving campaign following our successful acquisition of Empire Hotels, and so…

-I see.

-But that's no excuse for him smoking in my opinion. It's absolutely forbidden.

-So what do you think went wrong?

-Well that's very difficult to answer right now as he's still sedated. He will receive an official warning from the company and be asked to explain his actions. But not in his present condition. However, I'll be teaming up with Benito Pallotta in Human Resources on that, and he has assured me that this incident will be treated with the utmost severity.

-Okay, thanks again Francesca for your contribution. Let's catch up with Mutton at 11.30 by conference to clear up the situation about the sprinklers and kitchen equipment certification with Maintenance.

-Certainly, Mr. Conrad.

***

Six

Here we go again, that's the phone ringing, and this time it's the landline. If I didn't live in such a remote place I'd have had it taken out years ago. I've just sat down for my coronation on my throne of thrones. I always take my phone to the loo. You never know it could be another job call. When you work for a multinational you can't ever say no, not even when you're on the job! Oh, it's Aunt Dorothy. Her timing is impeccable as always….

-"Yeh, it's me Aunty Dot. …Have you got your hearing aid on?

-What's that? The apron? …Yes, I'm wearing it now. It was a lovely surprise for my ninetieth birthday. Have you seen the March picture on the Heritage Calendar I sent you? The Luton Hoo. I got it at the Heritage Open Day last year. The narcissus are beautiful, don't you think? It's not easy being ninety my dear nephew. My knee's playing up again and I'm having difficulty walking. I'm trying not to put my weight on my left leg. I don't think the new medicine is working either. It's getting me down. And I think it's making me a bit loose with my bowel movements. I have to empty my colostomy bag twice as often. It's all bulky and soft, not diarrhoea though. I'm sure it's the new medication. And I can't talk to your dad about it because he never listens; he'd tell me to go to the doctor's but I'm in too much pain to get in the car. He's never been able to deal with other people's problems. He just gives me advice about the things I already know. And it would take a week to get the doctor to visit me at home. What use is that? I might be dead in a week! The clinic's always interrogating me over the phone, and they know I'm hard of hearing. Anyway, at least the doctor did listen to me yesterday, and that made me feel a bit better. He asked me if the pain had got any better with the new medicine, and when I thought about it, no it hadn't, so he suggested upping the dose. Not being able to go out is depressing. But neighbours are wonderful. They leave my shopping at the door. And Roland does the big shop for me on Fridays. But I just feel so useless. Last year, I had to give up being an Abbey guide because I don't get free parking at the Abbey and it's too far for me to walk all that way across the common. I wrote a letter of complaint to the Bishop of St. Albans and he made a polite reply on headed Abbey paper informing me that I could have discount parking behind the Cathedral but that they needed all the spaces for guests who pay £5.50 a visit.

-But you've been doing the Abbey guide stuff for nearly 40 years, and for free!

-And now I've had to stop the Philharmonic Chorus too, because I can't stand up for all that time during rehearsals. I've got no social life, and people hardly ever call, and when they do it's to tell me that someone has died or been taken ill. Sorry, that's your old aunt complaining again. Sorry, sorry. I guess I'm a little depressed right now. Anyway, my next door neighbours look after me. Bindi always has a kind word but he's not much of a conversationalist.

-Isn't it Beele? A bindi is a red dot, Dot.

-You don't have to repeat yourself. I'm not deaf, you know. But I don't want to take more medicine if it's having this effect on my bowels. I've decided to try going back to my old medicine and see if it gets any better. I've still got a week's dosage. I do the injections myself. And with the new stuff, it's more complicated. This morning, I took the outer cap off, and then the inner one, but I couldn't see the needle inside. I don't know if it came away with the cap or something.
-Is that a needle-free injector you're using?
-I don't know what I'm doing wrong. So I thought that's it, back to the old medication. At least I can see the needles, and I've been doing it for years. That way, if my bowel movements become more solid again I know the reason. I'm not just increasing my dosage because the pain is no better. I can't go on like this. As soon as I put my weight down on my left heel I start to feel pain, so I have to lean on the other leg, and that's the one with the worn-out knee prosthesis. They won't do me another one because of my heart. I had the last one at 86. Anyway; I think I've had a good run with for my money with the NHS. That's three new knees, a colostomy bag and a double mastectomy. And before I was seventy, I'd never had an operation in my life! WE old folks certainly give them a run for their money. There I go complaining again. – Sorry dear. At least you listen to me. Well, I suppose I should think about making my mid-morning coffee.
-Have you decided what to have for lunch yet?

-Well, I've still got half a cheese and onion quiche from Waitrose, and I was thinking of boiling a potato or two. I might do two because they're quite small. I've got some frozen peas, so I could add a few of those too. It's a quick meal to make. I'm not really up for cooking today. It's been a cold and wet few days, and...

-Aunt, what's flowering in your garden at the moment?

-Well the honesty is everywhere, and where it shouldn't be too. It's in all the flower beds you know. It must have been all the wind we had last autumn. It sent the seeds into my roses. And the gardener hasn't been because of the weather, and he never does the tidying after he's finished, so I haven't called him for two weeks. But the grape hyacinths are beautiful under the hedgerow this year. They must have liked all the rain we had last winter. They're gorgeous. Well, what I wanted to say was that if I go back to my old medicine for a week, because I know that a day or two won't make any difference, then I'll know if that's the cause of all the extra bulk. I can bear the pain, but it's all that messing with the colostomy bag that gets me down.

-Well Aunt Dorothy, you're doing great. Tell me about the birds in the garden.

-You know, this season there haven't been many greenfinches.

-Are they nesting?

-Perhaps they've got enough food eating all the grubs, but there have been quite a lot of blue tits. They're such cheeky fellas.

-We have a cheeky blue tit too! Every morning, he cleans up the crumbs from…

-And you know what, there are a couple of starlings that have got the knack of hanging on to the feed box, so they're scaring off all the other birds. And they can be quite attractive when the sun catches them. They've got quite iridescent wings, and their numbers have been dwindling lately. But that's all you can say about them. For the rest they're pretty ugly.

-Well, they're certainly don't qualify for your song birds, do they?

-No, no…

-And what about the cats?

-Well my garden is a walkthrough for them! Ghastly beasts.

-And do you still shoo them away?-Well of course I can't run down the garden with the broom, but I do stand and wave at them from the bay window. Well, it's way past me coffee time. Thanks for putting up with me.

-Take care now, and call if you're feeling down.

-Bye love.

-Bye Aunt Dorothy."

***

Seven

Right I'm just in time to give Edo a quick call. I want to get to the bottom of all this homophobic nonsense with Giorgio. I'm not having my son grow up as a gay hater. He just doesn't realize how fascist it is out there. He lives a sheltered life at the hospital. The MILF-wives are the worst of all. Most of them I know from school don't work and spend most of their day ankle-biting on Facebook and Twitter. They all bitch about one another through subversive What'sApp groups. I'm a member of twenty-four groups for a class of thirty kids and I just haven't got time for all their crap. I work full-time in a high pressure job with a high level of responsibility. I abandoned the mum's "football trainer sucks group" at the start of last season, when Monica alluded to me having an affair with the coach. I wasn't having any of that. She's another one of those fat zeros who spends all her time trolling on social media. Anyway, I don't have a FB profile. Instagram is okay, because Giorgio has that. They're not dragging me down to their level. I've always wanted the best for myself, and will stop at nothing short of perfection. I should never have given up ballet. I was made for the stage. But having two science teachers as parents was not compatible with the arts, and after Gran died, God bless her, the resistance petered out. It was inevitable. My parents meted out love in return for top grades. That's why I want my son to be free to do what he wants. Because I wasn't. And that's why Giorgio gets unconditional love.

-"Edo, it's *Traumschwarz*!
-Ah my trusty steed, Francesca!
-There you go with your TS jokes.. Smart work, *Stormtrooper*! Had any epic battles today?
-No just you!

-You're just about right there. Are you preparing lunch? Because if you are, don't make a mess like yesterday. I'm having a shit day and I'm not going to tidy up after you again. And don't forget the wholegrain rolls from the organic bakery - the gluten-free ones. My latest intolerance tests have come back and they rate me borderline celiac. And Giorgio always has stomach aches too. We must look into that.
-Well, perhaps you could cut out have the freshly-squeezed lemon juice first thing in the morning with your double espresso and try eating some food. And no, I'm not having lunch. I've only just had breakfast.
-Look, I'm not going to argue with you about food. You know my stomach is always closed till mid-morning. I've got too much on my plate to entertain breakfast. The lemon juice is for my metabolism and I can't wake up without a double espresso. Make sure the rolls are fresh. Watch out for that shop assistant - she's always throwing in yesterday's bread if you take your eye off her for half a second. It's illegal but she keeps it under the counter. I've seen her do it. Anyway, I wanted to talk to you about something else. I've been getting wind of your homophobic slurs again from Giorgio. I don't want him to grow up with that.
-And I don't want him to grow up a sissy. It's bad enough that he's friends with Thomas. That boy's got weak wrists and he walks round with his hands permanently down his pants.
-But Thomas is top-scorer on the team this year. And his mother's my best friend. Chiara is a bit permissive, I

know, and I don't agree with him having oil-green highlights in his hair either. But he had a piercing at eight and his first tattoo at ten. For them it's normal.

-Well, he's a bad influence. So a few hard truths won't harm him. The boy's got to get the other side of the story if he's going to grow up balanced. I don't want a nancy-boy in my house. I'm not a fascist, but he's going to grow up with a strong sense of his masculine identity. That's what I think and I'm not changing my mind. It's bad enough that you go to a queer hairdresser.

-All hairdressers are gay. The ones that say they're not are in denial and are closet queens. Look at Romeo, my previous hairdresser. He was married, and he got caught with his pants down in the park. The police sent the arrest report to his home formally charging him with indecent exposure in public. Of course, his wife opened the post. That's normal. After that, he suicided. It might have taken prostitution off the streets, but it only moved the Ruby girls straight into Number 65, Via Oglettine, where they continue to have their sleaze parties. Protect the rich and shame the poor… just as before. The Italian way of taking prostitution beyond the streets is just another privilege granted. How convenient! And we all know which government brought in that law. And don't forget your fascist mayor – the one with exceptionally good taste in Brazilian *viados*! Anyway, Giorgio has his first girlfriend so you should be proud of that. You know it's Elisa. She's that beautiful tall blond girl and she's top of the class. So intelligent. I think he's really into her.

-Have you been watching Bollywood movies again? It's not appropriate to arrange Indian-style marriages for twelve year-olds in our culture. Isn't her father Romanian? Eastern Europeans, they all steal. They only joined Europe so they could take our money and get free access to our healthcare system. They're all alcoholics too. Believe me, I've seen plenty of them stretchered in at A&E. Broken legs from falling off ladders and then they're on sick leave for six months. All that plum brandy they put down the hatch sends their blood pressure through the roof. I can usually smell them in A&E before I see them!

-Christ, Edo! I don't believe you said that. You're a total racist monster. Andrei was born here. He's one of the cadet football team trainers and everyone adores him. And Elisa's mum is Giuseppina, who teaches at Giorgio's school. Despite my notorious hostility to teachers, her heart's in the right place and she's really great with the kids. I know she's not a genius otherwise she wouldn't have ended up a history teacher. But most importantly, it's Edo's first date, and she's Elisa mother, so don't spoil it.

-But isn't she Sicilian?

-This is going nowhere, so lay off Giorgio with the homophobia and all the rest of it, and don't forget the bread rolls. I won't see you later because I'm going to have an early night, so don't wake me. I'll leave your dinner in the fridge. All you have to do is heat it up in the oven 180°, twenty minutes should be enough..

-If you hadn't carried out a military jihad on microwaves, I would only need three minutes to heat it up! You know I'm exhausted when I get home after work.

-Look, I know you don't get food radiation or destroy the nutrients from a microwave, but an oven heats it up in a more uniform way, even if it takes longer. And it tastes better.

-Well, I'm a pragmatist and three minutes with hot edges and a lukewarm middle is fine by me after 10.00pm!

***

Eight

God, I'm dreading this next conference call with Conrad and the Stewart Mutton. Ever since Mutton made a pass at me last year at the Annual Conference - just before he passed out after downing three bottles of Bollinger - he's been particularly unpleasant to me. I could have whistleblown him for peer mobbing but he had to have his stomach pumped that night, and I felt sorry on him. And I should have seen it coming really. I mean the week before, he kept dropping in on my office with that baseball cap and goofy grin just to ask me absurd questions like which company made the top defibrillator in 2019. Of course, I haven't got a clue about which company made the top defibrillator in 2019! What a bore! He even asked me to sponsor him for the Smile charity fundraising run and never did it, claiming that he'd come down with a stomach bug the night before. I've always thought he was gay myself. But Babs did warn me! I'm just so slow on the uptake with guys coming on to me. I can see right through other people's motives when I'm out of the equation, but when the attention is directed at me, it goes straight over my head. I mean I got so little attention as I kid. I was the little nerd girl from the science family. We only ever exchanged facts at the lab bench (breakfast bar) based on empirically observable evidence, of course. "Mum, osmosis is happening in the moka, and it is precipitating an oily brown liquid with a hissy vapour that's condensing." "No, my dear, the liquid is exuding. Precipitation is when solids form…". "No mum, it's definitely precipitating, because it's spilling all over the floor." Although they were atheists, they sent me to catechism. Catechism for 'cattacomunist' kids… just so I wouldn't stand out as the devil child misfit! Religion is for the brain dead, they would say, but I wasn't ever allowed to repeat that. Thank God there was Gran. She didn't burden me with the moral responsibility of atheism. She was a devout Roman Catholic and she gave me hope. She taught me to be kind, always to be kind, and to forgive. And she didn't expect me to be perfect. She said I would always be a sinner in the eyes of the Lord anyway, so I might as well forget that perfection nonsense from an early age. And in any case I could confess, because God saw all my sins and I would be forgiven if I was truly repentant. Then it all went pear-shaped when Gran dropped dead during the Sunday Eucharist. Dad said it was just after the priest had popped the sacramental wafer onto her tongue, and nobody knew if it was the body - or the blood of Christ- that had actually choked her. I've never forgiven him for saying that. At least I've Gran to thank for being agnostic. So when Gran passed, I went bulimic, and rapidly declined into a fucked-up de-sexualised teenager – an awkward hybrid indulging in my own imperfection, terrified of sex because I felt unwanted, and compensating with top grades to expiate my craving for affection. That made me vulnerable and an easy target for the sex bullies. Wow! I deserve a medal for lucidity. Of course, I grew out of it eventually and now I never lose control, but those sexually depraved viruses have got their receptors out there and are always ready to hook onto me. There are two types of men I attract. Gays and cocksure philanderers. Neither are of much use to me. "Stewed Mutton" would like to think he belongs to the Latin-lover laymen's club, but he's out of control with the booze. I mean it's ruined his private life – his wife walked out with the kids last year – and his professional life will soon be following suit if he doesn't clean his act up. He's damned unreliable at the best of times, and you can't afford to be like that in a knowledge-based multinational like ours. As I was saying, sex is not a turn-on for me. I much prefer engaging intellect with the opposite sex. Ah, that's the director is ringing in..

.

-"Ah Mr Conrad, the only man in the entire company who's earned his capital C for culture! You must tell me about how the legacy of fascism survived in the immediate post war period. I'm fascinated by history.

-Francesca, call me Jeff. It's our second call today.

-Jeffrey, it's not easy being the only woman director here. The other directors don't take my work seriously. Female engineers are few and far between. But I know my job very well, and I don't intend to take responsibility for my male colleague's inadequacies. Mutton has no excuse for not answering my mails. If I'd been an HR Director, things would have been different. Female HR Directors are more accepted there than in our Department.

-I understand. As Mutton is not with us yet, let's try calling him to join our conference call…. Ah, that's him ringing in from his mobile now.

…..

-Mutton, you're late…. Okay, I understand you're at the site and a faulty hydraulic pump is causing problems with the excavation work. ..What's that? You can't get a decent line for the conference call? Francesca Scarpa is with us too. …Listen, I can't hear you properly .. Well move to a better place then. …Look, just stay on the mobile... Yes, that seems better now. …I want to know why the water sprinklers didn't activate, and more importantly, where's the conformity certification for the kitchen equipment? Francesca sent you four emails from Health & Safety Department. ….What do you mean you never received them? …..And how long have you been having problems with the server? …..Yes, I know Roberta's on maternity leave as well. And the temp? ….What, she's been off with a flu for 10 days? …What's that? You've been getting hacked again? ..What? The ad is back on the net about you selling automatic firearms using your company email?

That's absurd. We are a family destination resort, God forsake us! But we paid a fortune to get it removed! When was the certification last carried out for the water sprinklers and kitchen equipment? …What do you mean you didn't do it last year? …Central finance cut the budget? Okay, that's enough! Go back to the building site. I'll sort this with Francesca. But I want you at my office first thing on Monday morning at 9am.

-He's lying about the emails. These are his typical avoidance strategies – filling your head with unconnected wild claims in rapid flow - to throw off balance. Don't give in to him Jeffrey.
-This is a major headache, Francesca. We need to handle this very carefully. I don't think it's a good idea to tell head office about the missing certification. Otherwise, we'll both be looking for a new job. We need to make sure this incident is hushed up. Security staff mustn't talk to the press. Francesca, can you get our lawyers on to it? Perhaps we can take out an injunction, while we examine the case for the security offer's contributory negligence…. I'll find out about his sedation; I'm good friends with the hospital director. We have to act quickly. And remember, nothing written. Ah, and we need to speak to the Fire Chief about what to write as the cause of the fire. Can you do that?
-Of course, Jeff, leave it with me!"

***

Nine

I'm so glad the Director doesn't get involved in all that matey male stuff. Vaginas and soccer is about as much as there is to most of them, whether it's the doorkeeper or the Chairman of the Board. But Conrad seems different. And he's not gay. I'm sure of that because that leery left eye sometimes gets the better of him as he cranes his neck for a boob angle during our team meetings. And when he stoops over to pick up a cigarette stub outside the hotel reception, he rakes in a wide-angle sweep at my skirt split. Of course, men - Conrad included - are more self-contained when I'm on trouser days, or when I do my cloistered Clarisse act with that 8-inch wide Melania Trump chastity belt shored up under my ribcage. That always turns them off for a few days. Melania is a perfect example of a trussed up huss. And that tacky colonialist Out of Africa outfit of hers. How patronizing! What an insult to the Africans peoples. I mean it could at least have been khaki. Outrageous! We women are always being vetted for what we wear. That's why we have to countenance charm with austerity. And the higher up the ladder we get, the more it counts to dress for austerity. Look at all the world's genderless female Prime Ministers we've had: Thatcher, the Iron Lady, Theresa Maybot, and Angela "Mutti" Merkel - she's definitely the Mother of all Parliaments". But how drab! My other favourite Francydress decoy is the Miss Jean Brodie look where I go for a high-cut smock and plain chiffon scarf – tartan in the winter. Of course, I have to get my hair permed for that, but it certainly deals a death blow to my cleavage and the keeps the boys from perving for a while. Their super egos just can't hack it, and anyway most men's powers of persuasion amount to little more than a twig and berries. I mean take Richard Gere and Julia Roberts in Pretty Woman. It's an awful film. It's not romantic at all, and he doesn't have a seduction technique. It's just one *cliché* after another. The bottom line is that he's just too drop dead gorgeous to resist. And 99.9% recurring of you guys are not! Got it? Imagine if it had been Woody Allen instead of Mr Head Gere. You definitely wouldn't want to watch the film a second time, and probably not even a first one for that matter. Anyway, I know I can have any man I want! It's all about that subliminal quality of transforming unavailability into an art form. And I'd rather be a prudish Prime Minister than the Fake Frozen First Lady, that's for sure. My husband definitely has a point when it comes to Eastern Europeans.

Now Conrad has a hobby. He's doing a model reconstruction of Wellington's final assault of the Battle of Waterloo, and he painstakingly paints every soldier down to the very last detail, including the blood spats. He must be so patient. Men with hobbies. I admire them so much. At least, they sublimate their sexual desires. That's why they have self-control. That makes me wonder about Edo. He needs a creative outlet too… He doesn't really do anything but work. To be fair, he doesn't' have much free time. What with all the hours he spends down in the operating theatre, then he's on the wards, visiting patients during their recovery, reassuring them, and after that there's the admin and patient follow-up and the pre-op visits for special cases. I hardly ever see him really. And then all those night shifts. I mean that must exhaust him. He's a slave to his job. I never check up on him, not Edo. Testosterone abandoned him like a sinking ship years ago and nobody threw him a lifebelt. And I'm certainly not about to re-board the Titanic. You know, I can't even recall if we've been there since Giorgio was born. We women change when we become mothers. I was already in my early-thirties… and my career was in full swing. I took it all in my stride. No looking back. Just in case he gets a bit curious, I like to give him the odd errand on his mornings off.

***

Ten

Ah it's Chiara.. Wonder what she been up to this time? I can't speak to her now, we're in full-blow crisis management. Oh well, just a couple of minutes….

-"Chiara, everything okay?
-Franci, I've got to tell you.. This is incredible! I mean, I was at our Bakery this morning and Angus was there too.

You know Angus the mangled biker? Well he asked me to have a coffee with him at our bar.

-No Chiara, you didn't have coffee with him, did you? He's only after your *Gräfenburg*-spot. Well I hope you told Angus to take the G out of his name and go and swallow himself!

-No listen, you know I'm always up for a laugh. We were stood at the bar and he was there in his jogging bottoms so I just couldn't help doing the 80cm sideways glance and noticing he was getting a bump. It was like a scene from The Gladiator. There he was wielding it in full view, and shamelessly. He asked me if I wanted to go up to his place for sex, right there! It was his day off and he was just coming back from the gym. So, ..

-No Chiara, stop there! Too much detail… I'm working, and that hopeless drunk colleague of mine, Mutton Chops, has landed me in the shit big time. After his wife left him, and petitioned for custody of the kids, he hit the bottle like there's no tomorrow. Anyway, he's fucked up again, because we didn't renew the certification for the kitchen equipment or water sprinklers this year. He's dropped me in the shit by saying that he never got my mails asking him to do the maintenance, the finance department in the shit by saying they cut the budget, and the whole company in the shit if we get caught out for not having certification. We've got to do a major cover up! I've rung the lawyers and they're taking out an injunction to make sure the security guard keeps *stumm*. But you know what security are like when you stick them before a camera. They'll do anything for a bit of attention. Luckily, our injured guard is not mutilated or anything, just a crispy bacon ear. Anyway, the HR boss, you know Benito the Psycho, has sent an official warning letter about his smoking at the scene of the incident, and we're going to threaten to sue for the damage caused to the hotel. That should be enough to make him lie low for a while. Of course, it won't go down very well with the trade union rep. A few thousand Euros should keep him happy. Then, the director just happens to be old friends with the consultant surgeon who's looking after him, so they're going to keep him sedated till Tuesday. Frankly, I'm worried about my position. Someone will have to foot the bill for this one? ….Sorry to interrupt, I just had to get that off my chest..So did you go back to his flat?

-Of course not, Franci! I'm not that desperate, even if he has a cute butt and that *Noémie Lenoir* tapered stocking merits further investigation. Well, all the time we were at the bar, I was texting with the other Francesca, so I told her to call me in exactly five minutes and invent a major catastrophe. Her timing was tremendous.

-That's playing with fire. You know I'm superstitious about those kinds of things. Never tempt destiny. It always gives you what you ask for, and more.

-So Franci, we literally got to his door and the phone rings. She was blasting away - in that high pitched voice of hers so he could hear every word - that her car had broken down in the middle of nowhere and she couldn't miss her appointment… unbelievable. I shrugged my shoulders pathetically, did a quick 180° heel spin and disappeared saying it was an emergency and we would catch up soon. She's been a great friend since we had it out over her trolling me about my glittered *Jimmy Choo* ballerines. Do you remember? We both bought a pair last time we went shopping in Milan? You know I just don't care. I'll do literally anything. I've been like this since I had my first period. I'm never going to change. I've been splitting my sides ever since and just had to call you.

-You're my totally crazy best friend. Being a mum just made no impact on you, did it? I admire you so much. It turned me into a dragon overnight. Did you give him your number?... Oh no, I've just got a text from Giorgio. He's not feeling well at school. He's got stomach ache again. I have to text him back. Sorry, bye. Speak soon. Love you…

"Giorgino, mama is here. Is it one of your usual stomach aches? Are you doing a maths lesson again? If it's really bad, tell the teacher you need to go to the nurse. But try to sit it out. I'll call you at lunch break to see how you are. Mama loves you, be brave! PS keep me posted."

***

Eleven

'Hi…'

'Hey'

'What you up to?'

'Nothing much

> *Just browsing the chat room'*

'Live in the city?
It says you're 1.2 km from me
I'm near the pool'

> *'I'm by the hospital'*

'Good. I work nearby
Married?'

> *'Committed*
> *You?*

'Married'

> *'Good*
> *I only go for married guys*
> *Hairy?'*

'I've got a beard
You can still see a bit of my face.

> *'Funny!*
> *I love sweaty!'*

'Hairy and sweaty, then'

> *'Fun and games?'*

'No, just safe sex'

> *'So that's Vanilla, then*
> *One scoop or two?*
> *Any face pics?'*

'No face, dick and legs'

....

'Hmmm, swarthy and nice choker
> *What you up to?'*

'Your pictures?'

'Here, how about these?'

......

'Wow, do you work out?
I'm free till 2pm'
                            'Gym
        You married guys are always so eager!'
'Ok maybe next time, sorry'
                'Hey, if you'll be Yogi
                I'll be your Honey Pot'
'Is that a yes?'
                          'Of course,
            Give me your number'
'No phone numbers'
                'What's your address?'
'Don't do addresses'
                    'Free for coffee?'
'Now? Where?'
                'The bar on the corner
        Next to Ayurveda herbal store
                        Ten minutes?'
'How will I recognize you?'
          'I'm the "lemon tart" of course!
              Bring your vitamins
              I love to swallow.'

That was a nightmare. I haven't got the faintest idea about this chatting game. I'm going to have to improve my technique, work out a strategy. Lemon tarts and vitamins, what's all that about? Maybe vitamins is another word for blue diamonds? But lemon tarts? I wonder if they sell them at the Ayurvedic health store. Thank God, I've got Renato in General Medicine. I'll quiz him on that one. He's a goldmine of information. He recommended 50mg first time round - 25 might not be enough and I don't want to be letting the team down! If it's too much, next time I can take the throttle off and coast on a 25mg. But what if it is too much? I've got good blood pressure and no problems with the old ticker. The ECG at the Cycle Ergometer Test showed I had the heart of 40 year old. But that was a while back, come to think of it. At least five years out of date. Ren said to get a newspaper so I can walk "discreetly" to the hospital just in case, but once I'm in my hospital gown it won't matter. He said it wears off after an hour or so, so there shouldn't be a problem. Just enough time to dip the "bread finger in the soft boiled egg", he said! Shit that reminds me. Must text Franci about the rolls.

"Franci, didn't get to the bakery before closed. Long call with Oncology Dept. Admin issues. Got to be at work early for meeting. Speak later or CU tomorrow. Stormtrooper!"

"ST, Having a shit day. Need rolls for Giorgio's dinner. He's got stomach troubles again. Will sort it. TS"

She always calls me ST when she's pissed off with me!

※※※

Twelve

This is too deep for me. I've spent my whole professional life in a sheltered prison. I'm essentially a hospital technician, the one that has to set up all the parameters. Then I'm the hospital psychotherapist – a sort of emotional life support machine: I do pre-op prep-talks, resuscitation, post op wake-ups, pain management, quick tours of the wards with the consultants, and the odd Goodbye and God bless. It can get a bit hectic in intensive care at times, but I've always got the nurses and auxiliary to do all the dirty work. I've got all the responsibility wheeling them in for the op, but once they're on the chopping board it's Game Over! The surgeons get all the glory. I just can't hack this routine anymore. I think I'm starting to hate my job, either that or myself. I've been doing it almost thirty years. Day in day out, all the same stuff really, apart from the latest drug a pharmaceutical company is pushing, and occasionally a bit of new machinery to play with. For the rest, it's procedure, protocols and report-writing. I hate them. If I'd have known that thirty years ago, I'd have gone for a position as a local council administrator. Most of them get their mothers-in-laws to fetch their croissants for breakfast and swipe their attendance badges at the same time. They don't even get to work before 10.30. On the upside, I do get plenty of thank you notes and presents, of course. That's a nice trip for my ego. Old Bea is tops – she bring me homemade pasta for me every year just before Easter, *lasagnette*, made with eggs from her own free range chickens. That's special. And last week, the Ugandan woman, she gave me that shamanic healer's rattle… she said I'd healed her sprit. It was a family heirloom, her grandfather had been a witch doctor, I think. All a bit borderline for me; I'm a scientist after all. For the rest of the time, the hospital is just a grotesque circus of incestuous sycophants licking up to their superiors for their next pay rise. Then all of a sudden, you're overlooked for a promotion by someone 10 years your junior and that's it - second Game Over. The rest is tedium, nudging your way towards a pension and trying to shake off depression creeping up on you.

Perhaps, I should just go home, have a quick jerk off and then head for work. This is the worst ten minutes of my life. I've probably been stood up anyway. I haven't felt like this since I was sat before the jury for my thesis defense. I'm getting palpitations…

Come on Ed, wise up, give yourself a chance …. take some of that advice you use on your patients. How about a deep breath? Release it slowly through your mouth, and then in again through your nose, always three times. It's going to be fine. .. Phew, that's better. Ren did say that I could get quite a rush off the Viagra, especially if I had an empty stomach. But Jesus, I've got palpitations throbbing away in my ear drums right now, and my nose and eyes are burning too. Of course, I haven't eaten, it works better on an empty stomach. And my mouth's dry. Better take a fresh breath pearl.

-"Stormtrooper, right?
-Yes that's me.
-Lemon Tart, but call me Fiore. Wow, you've caught the sun.
- Had a bit of a stroll in the park, earlier. I'm Marcello. Fiore, what can I get you? I'm going to have an *espresso*.
-*Macchiato*, no sugar. Marcello, nice name. But I can see why they call you Stormtrooper. The Star Wars Saga. George Lucas right?
-You've got it. My wife got this Stormtrooper model of George Lucas for Giorgio a few years ago, and said it looked like me. The name's stuck ever since. She's totally in love with him. She even called our son, Giorgio, after him. Sorry perhaps not a good idea to mention my …
-No, not at all…Great hair and great beard. Groomed and thick, and peppered with a bit of silver. Sexy. Really suits you. In this day and age, most guys think they either have to look like an Islamic terrorist or an illiterate Amish Anabaptist. Hipsters are excluded from this equation because of their dress sense, of course, and they…
-Here's the coffee. You're in great shape too. Blond, tanned, and you've got youth on your side. Wow! if only I were your age again. And your jumper. …Now I know why you call yourself Lemon Tart.
-No you don't, but you'll find out soon. Shall we go?

-Just let me pick up my lightsaber! It's by the cash till.
-This is your first time, isn't it?
-Well, let's just say I'm not a regular at this game…
-Ready for the epic battle?
-"May the force be with you"…but "be careful not to choke on your aspirations"!
-What?
-Never mind, something Darth Veda said, just joking!"
-No doubting you, just about as cocksure as they come!"

***

Thirteen

-"Hi Benito, It's Franci here. Need to talk to you about some HR Training.
-Before we start, just remember we haven't got a budget for this Francesca. So what can I do for you?
-Listen Benito, we've got to do something about the alcohol abuse in this company. Random testing, maybe straight after lunch? Conrad agrees with me.
-No way, Franci, you're crazy. We spent all the training budget for this year on your "Raising the Bar for Safety Awareness" course, and to be blunt, it didn't get us very far with the security staff, did it?
-Come on Benito. We need this. There's no discipline and alcoholism is a real liability, quite frankly. We've got to face this issue sometime.

-Well you know what I think. These guys are as thick as two short planks and no amount of training will wake them out of their dreams. Half of them think they're going to take over from Dwayne Johnson in the next San Andreas "snuff the world movie" and the other half can't even spell their own names. You have to ask them every single question twice. "What's your name beefcake?" And they go all starry-eyed and just grin back at you and they say nothing. So you ask them again, and when it finally gets through that you're actually asking them a question, they answer you with a question, "What's that, are you asking me my name?" Unbelievable! By which time you just say, "Forget it, just follow me".

-You're such a cynic Benito. But come on, you're supposed to be the guru of self-betterment…

-Lay off it, Francesca. Charm won't work this time. I'm a fascist. My grandfather was a fascist. My father was a fascist and so am I. All you can do with these guys is give them orders and shout at them. The more you yell, the better. If you want them to do something, make them run. Kick arse big time and they'll do it. They're all pretty good guys really. Eager to please, low self-esteem, and once they respect you, they're at your beck and call. So forget the random alcohol testing. There would be no-one left in the Maintenance Department, if you had your way.

-Precisely!

-Oh, Come off it. Francesca. You've really got it in for Mutton. He's been through a difficult breakup, and he's fighting depression. Show some compassion.

-Compassion? My fucking job is on the line cos' of that prick! You guys are all the same. You just all stand up for each other, wallowing in your ignorance. You're all spineless. Fuck the lot of you.

-Hey, take it easy. Look, your procedures don't get anywhere with these guys, that's all I meant. What man in his right mind would open a safety door, knowing that there's a fire inside with a fag lit in his hand?

-A man, a genius, and our security guard!

-Ok, so what's your mission, this time? The greater good of the company? Give me a break! But that's you through and through Franci. Identify with the company's highest goal, make yourself a martyr for it and stuff the workers. That's your only mantra. Hasn't the mirror started to crack yet? And let me tell you another thing, nearly all the security staff have become cocaine addicts since you introduced that fucking electronic sign-off procedure of yours. They don't even have time to go to the shitter now! They do shifts on a six-day week and with a minimum 26 hrs contracts, so they not even on the minimum wage. What do you expect?

-I'm an engineer and I expect the job to be done properly. I find solutions to problems. I certainly don't make them.

-That's bullshit, and you know it. You don't have to sell your talents to me. I might be a fascist and I like things to stay the way they are, so I'm on the back foot when it comes to change, which might sound strange for a HR Director. But procedures, audits, reporting.. it just stresses us all out. You've got to stay human if you want to survive.

-When did a fascist ever stay human? You're off your planet. Anyone who breaks the rules, and they're out in your book. Last week, you fired a hotel cleaner because she was "caught red-handed" you said, with a bottle of company mineral water in her backpack. Was is still or sparkling, Captain America? I mean she was only nineteen. Where's the humanity in that? I go for knowledge-driven change. You're still living in the feudal age.

-And you're a corporate Nazi, Francesca, and you can't even see it. You'll screw anyone if it fits with the company's motto. And you've had more jobs than we've got workers in this company. I've been here for nearly thirty years and I love my job. Rules are rules, and these kids need to learn discipline. And we all know why you had to leave your last job....

-It certainly wasn't for philandering. Where were you when your father was on his death bed?

-You bitch!

-Go and fuck yourself!"

***

Fourteen

-"Fior, why is a Viagra called a Blue Diamond?

-Look at your boner, it's still hard as a rock. Diamond .....hard... rock...right?

-Am I so out of the picture?
-Well your lexicon is a little out of date, but you certainly know how "to grope for trout in my peculiar river"! And that "holy poker" of yours ... it takes some beating. Are you going to have a shower, then? The green towel is for you.
-No, I'll have one at work.
-At work?
-What's the time? Shit, five to two? I've got to run.
-Is this a one off?
-Of course not.
-Hmm, not so sure. Speak on chat, then?
-Right, sounds good.
-At least try to be convincing. How about a kiss?
-Sure....
-....Bye then.
-Bye, let's catch up soon!"

***

Fifteen

-"Chiara, I've just lost it with Benito the Psycho in HR, and I can't get in touch with my husband. Christ, that bastard is a real woman hater. He insinuated that I had lost my last job because I'd had an affair. Everyone knows that when the company was taken over, the Health & Safety Department got axed. I'm definitely going for an international position next time round. Can't

stand this provincial hell hole any longer. All the gossip! Maybe Amsterdam.
-Come on Franci, did he really say that?
-Not exactly, but he knew it, that's for sure.
-Well, you did fall for the Head of Finance in a big way when were in Rome; you were there on your own with Giorgino; I don't blame you, I'd have done far worse. But you can't have secrets these days, what with the internet and professional networking communities. Wasn't it the HR guy that shopped you up to the CEO at your last company? What is it with HR managers and their moral crusades, anyway? It's pure hypocrisy! They're all at it.
-That's as may be, but I went further. I let slip that I knew he was actually fucking with his secretary when the hospital called to say his father was dying.
-No, Franci! Brilliant. You've got a sharp tongue. I bet that put him in his place. Good on you. I admire you. Anyway, didn't Edo forgive you? That's all in the past now.
-Well, he did, yes. But I haven't forgiven myself for it.
-Look Franci, you can't change it anyway. What's passed is past. You just have to live with it. You've got a great husband, a great kid, a fab home and a top career, all in your home town. Everyone envies you. You're a self-made woman. You knock spots of all of us.
-Yes, but I'm having a shit life. I've got money and I've got power, and friends like you, but I've never even stopped to ask myself if this is what I want. I mean it's all just happened. I don't have a clue who I am. I'm totally

externally referenced, you see, and my life is as phoney as *Mulino Bianco* biscuit ads.

- Well, we're all the product of our upbringing. Don't be so hard on yourself. You had a good education, got great grades, have people skills and knew how to get on in life. What more could you ask for? You're a great example to all of us.

-No, Chiara, I'm just a product. End of story. That bastard even had the nerve to call me a "Corporate Nazi". Listen, I've got to go, I can feel a migraine coming on.

-Okay sweet, rest up this weekend, and try not to judge yourself.

-The weekend never comes! I've still got to do the sushi team-building lunch with my colleagues, then my nails, gym and hair. I can call my trainer to cancel the gym. I'm not up for that. And I have to pick up Giorgio from his football training at 6.30. Thank God, I've got my Brufen 600 with me. That should get me through the afternoon.

-Let me know how you get on with the sushi?"

Oh, she's gone... I wouldn't like to be in her shoes right now. Poor girl. When I had Thomas, and then Matilde, I stopped working and never went back. I've got my own money and my husband's too. He's a top dentist so we definitely don't need two incomes. Of course, I have no problems selling his miniature Buddha statues that he makes from the WAGS' veneers. They go for a fortune. I got nearly €3000 for the statuette he made from Georgina Rodriguez's cast-offs. Next week, we've got Ronaldo's mother, Maria Dolores dos Santos Aveiro, as well. I've asked Paolo to do a special edition resin composite of Padre Pio for that. She's a strict Roman Catholic, so I don't think it would be appropriate to do a statue of Buddha. Of course, they don't get to know about it. It's all hush hush; we sell by word of mouth. Paolo's so smart; he takes a selfie with all of them, and hangs it in his Hall of Fame in the waiting room. We don't need any more publicity than that. Ronaldo even gave him an autographed football last time. Of course, that's locked in the cabinet with the dentures exhibits, otherwise one of the WAGS would have pilfered it long ago!

***

Sixteen

-"Renato, are you at the meeting yet?
-Not yet. Why?
-Cover for me, I'll be a few minutes late. Listen I've got a permanent disability here.
-Are you with your mother-in-law? Has she had an accident?
-No, don't take the piss. I've got BDS, "blue diamond syndrome", it's crippling me. 50mg is far too high.
-Sorry, it's not a great line. You can't have had much action in the past ten years then! Not that I've ever needed it myself. I'm in great shape for sixty. As toned as ever…you should have taken up triathlon with me.

-Who are you kidding? You've just gone from erectile to neuronal dysfunction in less than a second. You've got a knack for that!

-Fuck off you touchy bastard, what was she like? Did you meet on chat? I bet I've already done a nice turn with her.

-I wouldn't bank on that, mate, but I'm pretty impressed.

-Come on Prince Charming, who's your Tinderella then? I hope she's not over forty. Forty is about the right age. By then, they've had plenty of disappointment, and their hormones are peaking…

-No, I mean the Viagra. Powerful stuff! I was getting pulsatile tinnitus while we were having coffee at the bar, and that was before it knew I was about to play Jack in the Box, and now it's thumping away in my boxers like Roger Rabbit with the hump! I'll never be able to sit through the next two hours with the trade union reps. It will be agony. And I've got an operation scheduled for 4.30 in the afternoon!

-Cold water rinse in the bidet and you'll be fine. Oh, by the way, did you get a paper to cross the road with? I want to check the line up for tomorrow's game.

-Fuck off, Renato. I'm dressed like Lieutenant Columbo. It's pissing down out here!

-See you in a couple of minutes. We're all having coffee at the bar.

-Don't breathe a word, or you'll be needing more than a Pfizer for your next fix, believe me!

-Don't worry, being with this lot is like being confined in the Béguinage!"

Five missed calls from *Traumschwarz*. Oh shit, don't what to speak to her now; better to say I forgot my phone, and had to dash home for it. I'll text her.

"Sorry missed your call. Forgot my mobile. Everything okay? About to go into meeting. Text me".

***

Seventeen

Sushi or not sushi? Didn't Yoko Ono, the Sweet Swan of Japan, sing about that in one of her songs? But seriously, what do we know about the Japanese? When I think about it, we've got them to thank them for household goods, electronic devices and cars, kimonos, fans, and a huge amount of nuclear fallout from Fukushima! But as Europeans, we know practically nothing about their culture. We think it can all be boiled down to geishas and samurais, and tea parties. Unless we're consuming it ravenously, we haven't got a clue. And that's why all the Chinese have traded in their "Fu King" takeaway licenses for the "Misohapi" sushi bar franchises. And the Chinese can't even be bothered to learn to say Arigatò! Oh, that double dose of Brufen has got me in a spin again, but at least the migraine's passing. It's just not my day, is it? Let me call Babs.

-"Babs, who's taking the sushi order today? Just get me some the sushi without the rice, I'm not very hungry.
-That's the *sashimi* then? Your usual?
-Oh yes, Babs, can you take care of it? It's the assortment box that comes with the heart-shaped avocado slices.
-We've done it already, Francesca. Come and join us."

My guys really are the best. They take care of me! I'm so lucky to have them, I've got a real knack for team-building! That reminds me, I've got to call Giorgio. He's having another one of his funny turns with his stomach…

-"Giorgino, it's mummy. Are you okay sweetheart? ….Well I'm glad you're feeling better now, but you didn't text me? You mustn't do football training if you're not well…. But you don't sound well. Your voice is trembling…. What, you're angry? ……You got a bad grade in your Maths again? But we pay for you to have extra tuition…. What do you mean, it was your homework this time? I did that for you. It was so easy, simple algebra. I just don't understand why you don't get it….. Anyway, don't worry, we'll talk tonight. If you're sure you're feeling better, you can do football, okay? Mummy loves you. Bye now, kisses."

Shit, I knew it. It's that bitch of a Maths teacher at school again. She's given Giorgio another bad grade for his homework. She's always upsetting him. You know she's got no patience with the kids. She's an Aquarius like me.

She thinks outside the picture, and she's unconventional, which makes her interesting as a person. And given the right environment, Aquarians are capable of exceptional humanity. She should be doing scientific research or managing international aid projects abroad, or something like that. Teaching Maths to twelve year olds is way below her status. And when frustrated, we Aquarians are often uncompromising and aggressive and that's no good for a emotionally sensitive boy like Giorgio. Anyway, I'm going to speak to the parents committee about it. She's not going to turn my son into an emotional wreck at such a delicate age. The difference between the two of us, of course, is that my ascendant is in Taurus, which grounds me and makes me a good mother. She must be an ascendant Leo, which accounts for egocentricity, and lack of sympathy. And Babs said she had a friend who's Aquarius ascendant Leo, and that was her down to a tee. Spot on again Francesca! When you're a scientist like me with a passion for astrology, it's hard to get it wrong, really.

But the guys never have much to say for themselves during team lunches! I know astrology's not football, but it's interesting to analyse people using alternative science-based knowledge, isn't it? I also got to ask Marco how's Anna been since we moved her to Hotel Reception? That's my natural empathy coming out again. I can't keep it in, even if it could be perceived as a weakness in a male-dominated workplace. I've still got to work on that part of myself. Compassion in the workplace is one of my big motivators. Just got to control it better. Benito wanted to fire her. But I put a stop to that. Anyway, he said she was doing fine, but that she missed our Team and reception work was boring. Poor Anna, we just couldn't keep her here, not after her husband got the job as a reporter for the local daily. I mean she had access to all our personal files and sensitive information with Health and Safety. We couldn't risk that. Good job we spotted their celebrations on Facebook. Babs is my top secret agent. Oh, is that the time, already? I've got an appointment with Mr Conrad.

***

Eighteen

Should be a couple of hours before I have to wake the patient. Still, quite a sizeable mass, despite the chemo. Inflammatory Breast Cancer. Today's operation is conservatory. It's still in the relatively early stages. These are the worst moments in my professional life. The ones that get through the filter. How can you not think about her life? She's only thirty, married, two young kids. There's no justice to it. It doesn't matter how much you've been trained about where to draw the line with emotional involvement, in some cases, you just don't have a barrier, and Rebecca is one of them. I've seen so many types of cancer and probably read equally as many - if not more - explanations about its causes. But if you want to know what the outcome will be when the word "malignant" appears in your pathology report, then we open you up to the world of conjecture, probability and treatment protocols. It's a bit like spinning the wheel of fortune. I've met and counselled many patients too, and they often say a period of prolonged stress was a major part of their lives just before their illness. But what is stress? Attempting to define it is like walking into a minefield of subjective impressions – trying to rationalise the unrelenting conflict between what our life is and what it ought to be. When we hold up the messy track record of experience against our paradigm of perfection, our dreams are suddenly shattered. We are told to expect so much of ourselves, and reality just can't bear us out on that. And we don't want the pain of seeing through the looking glass. Day after day, we're pushed to the limit, living in chaos, chasing that all-elusive concept of time. Time that there's never enough of, and time that never existed. As a consequence, we're all stressed. We all have our favourite one-liners: "Don't stress me!", "Are you stressed out or something?" "You must be stressed", "My job stresses me", "People stress me", "Life stresses me", "You stress me". Look inside yourself, I say, because it's not out there. It's you. It's who you are and the way you are; that's stress. At the end, there's a price to pay, and some people simply cope with stress better than others.

Look what happened to me, when Francesca was fucking around with the jerked up finance manager. He was so far up his own arse, we wouldn't have even been able to flush him out with colonic irrigation. And I would never have known, if Francesca hadn't blurted. It was a Sunday afternoon, and we were sat there waiting for the football round up with Giorgio, and she triumphantly announced "It's over"! I didn't say a word. I froze. My heart was pounding and my whole body started shaking, then the cold sweat. But I just stared at the TV, transfixed. Then they left for Milan. I didn't flinch. By Tuesday, I'd got shingles with a fever, a fiendish headache and I couldn't bear looking at the light, so I called up sick and stayed home for a week. I never answered her messages or calls. I just stayed in bed, festering. Then she reappeared the following Saturday morning with Giorgio and her suitcases, and announced "I've left my job". That was it. No explanations, no apologies. Cold silence interceded. Of course, I took her back, why wouldn't I? I was in my early fifties with a young boy to bring up. A family man. And we've talked about it since, I dare say. I've never forgiven her though. We negotiated by degrees from that point on, passing from curfew, to truce before finally signing the peace treaty that's still in place today. Yes, our own Wilsonian fourteen point peace plan that negated every right to self-determination - and that's where we are now - as long as no one upsets the apple cart. Anyway, I take my share of the blame. I've always been a steady, dependable and trusting kind of person, happy to do my part, never asked too many questions. Of course, I had my fun when I was younger. But when I decided to start a family, I put it all behind me. And Francesca was right, I never took much notice of her after Giorgio arrived. I didn't adapt to her changing needs, she said. I took it for granted that she was a mother, and she was doing what she wanted. But she ignored me too, and I resent that. We've never been able to express our feelings to each other. So I buried my head in my work, and she did basically the same wearing Giorgio as her designer label. No regrets, then? I've never really understood why she left her job though. But that's enough of me.

Rebecca, I'm getting too sentimental again. Sleep peacefully. Rebecca, if you're listening in on me, you're in with a fighting chance. Good luck to you.

***

Nineteen

Couldn't wait to get that lunch over and done with. Only Babs was pro-active. Of course, society has changed, but it's still hard being the only female director. And they do appreciate my insistence on vocational training courses; it's so important with all the new ISO standards, procedures to follow and guidelines to implement. And team-building is an essential part of that. Then, I 'm always telling them that if you put your heart into it, your head will follow. And in all fairness, my guys are on top of their work, and to my credit, my department scored highest on the employee satisfaction survey in the whole group last year. I gave them all a star for that. And it will be the same this year too. Understandably, they're less keen when it comes to professional development plans (PDPs), especially now we've linked them to their annual bonus entitlement. But that is definitely the right approach in a knowledge-based company like ours; we're at the top of our industry and we want to stay there. But most importantly, it's our way of keeping them in check, and weeding out the lazy ones. I suppose Benito does have a point there. And he's right about prejudice too. Basically, the guys don't want to take orders from a woman on a building site, especially with me in my matching yellow jack boots and protective helmet. I mean I'm hardly Bob the Builder, and for them it's just not macho. Chiara said they were doing a "Hammer and Pliers" twinset in autumn yellow at Accessorize if I wanted to go for the full complement! She's really takes the piss! Well, the most important thing is that the guys respect me for who I am. I fought tooth and nail to get here and they know it. And another thing, I changed jobs and cities five times in my first ten years, a happy medium by most engineers' standards, but most of the employees here are still going home at lunchtime so that mum can changes their Huggies! Apart from Anna, we've had no staff turnover in my department in the five years since I joined the company, and hers was an internal transfer for political reasons. Of course, there are still a few scores to settle with my deputy, Raffaele – I call him Riff-Raff, but once I've got shot of him, we'll have a dream team. He was hankering after my job, and after he didn't get it; he started a smear campaign against me. I bet he was the one who spat the dummy about my affair. To his credit, he's the most punctual member of staff when it comes to early afternoon badge-swiping. Anyway, revenge is sweet and it's just a question of time. I give him nothing to do, and by ten in the morning he's bored out of his tiny mind. Serves him right, and there's no way he should have a 40K company car, now that he only commutes 10 kilometres a day. I'd like Maintenance to take him. Once all this shit is over with Mutton, I'll get straight on to that. At least there, he'd be some use in developing procedures. They haven't got any right now, that's for sure. Stew doesn't even know where he is at the moment. Anyway, good job Mr Conrad cancelled the 1.30pm meeting, now I'm in good time for my manicure.

Christ, that was painful! And it's bleeding everywhere. I've torn my nail again. Always in a hurry. That'll teach me! ……Oh fuck, she's closed! And she didn't call me. She's such a dipstick. What the fuck am I going to do now?
-"Gemma! It's me Franci. Where in the fuck's name are you?
-I'm at the vet's with Lolita. She swallowed a chicken bone, and nearly choked to death. She's on the operating table now.
-What happened? Everyone knows you don't give chicken bones to dogs! … I'm sorry, please don't sob, try to get a hold of yourself. Sorry, really I am.
-She stole my chicken korma and buffalo mozzarella sandwich while I was cutting out Marianna's in-growing toenail, and next second she was honking up and railing like a possessed donkey. Poor Lolie, I've never had any luck with cockapoos. You remember Josie got electrocuted when Antonella accidentally dropped the hairdryer in the dog grooming sink. And that was

supposed to be her birthday treat. She never got to eat her cake. And I'd had it specially made at the Dog Cake Bakery. I knew I should have gone for a pedigree shih-zhu this time. They're smaller and would never have been able to jump up and swipe the sandwich.
- Listen, listen she'll be fine, I'm sure. When can I see you? I can't last the weekend without a manicure. I snapped my wedding ring finger nail backwards as I was getting out of the car on my way to your boutique, and it's torn into my nailbed.
-Is it still bleeding?
-Now it's oozing.
-Have you got any silk wraps?
-Well not here.
-Are you on your way to Angelo's for your hair after me? He doesn't do nails but he keeps silk wraps for an emergency. He can do you a temporary job until tomorrow, I'm sure. I can fit you in before I open at quarter past nine. I'll do the final touches. Is that okay?
-You're my guardian angel. See you tomorrow at 9.15. Give Lillie a cuddle from me when she comes round.
-Lolie.
-Sorry, sorry, sorry, Lolie!"

***

Twenty

-Giorgio, can you get Angelo for me? It's urgent. Tell him it's Francesca, Franci! Thanks….

-Angelo!

-Franci, everything okay?

-No, I'm early. Listen I severed my nail. Wedding finger again! Gemma said you've got silk wraps.

-Of course! We've got everything you could ever dream of Calamity Jane! Trust me. But, it will have to be Tristan, I'm too squeamish for that sort of thing. And we've got your D&G nail polish too. I keep a few essentials from The Nail Lacquer collection: petal, nude and drama. In the hair boutique, I do nude, of course, because I don't want to upstage you ladies with anything more sassy. You're not ready for that. I keep dahlia in my private collection at home and that goes down a treat when I'm out tranny chasing with the boys. They really go crazy for my ginger tom beard. Anyway, do nude, then little Gem can sort you out tomorrow, okay?

-Drama is my mood today, but you know best. Listen, can I come now? I'm about five minutes away, and I still want my mèche afterwards.

-I've got Lorena booked in for the High Fliers' Salon upstairs, but if you don't mind hobnobbing it with the peasant farmers' wives, we can sort your nail out downstairs in the charity canteen, then after, you can come up for your castor oil and red onion root therapy before we start "mèching" about with you! And before you ask, they're organic red from Tropea. But you might have to wait a few mins for that. You know what it's like here on a Friday. It's like doing auditions for "MILF - the Musical"! I promise we'll have a coffee together and a

chin wag, okay? Can't wait to get my hands on all that sumptuous honey hair of yours!
-Angelo…
-Franci?
-Go and wax your pole, will you! All that honey talk is making me puke!
-Ooh Miss Sourpussy, if you hadn't severed your nail you'd be scratching my eyes out. Meeeow!

***

Twenty-One

"Daniele, you're right... I should have been at the gym half-an-hour ago. You've already texted me six times? ….Daniele, I'm so sorry. I've had a major crisis. I snapped off a finger nail, and it bled so much I nearly went to A&E. I meant to call you to cancel…. I've had a migraine since this morning too, but then this happened. Can we do a catch up lesson at the beginning of next week? ….What's that? You still have to debit the lesson? ….The rules say that you have to cancel before 6:00pm on the day before? But it was an emergency! Can't you fit someone else in?.. Okay, okay, you're right. It's too late …. The lesson should be happening now. Can we do an extra-long lesson on Monday? … You're free from 3.30 to 6pm? How about 4.30pm? I should be able to get off early on Monday…. Yes of course. If there's a problem, I'll let you know first thing…. Yes, before nine, otherwise

I can't cancel. Right, got it.... Keep pumping too! See you on Monday."

I really don't think Virgin Active can make me pay for that cancelled lesson. I mean it's a benefit. All the Directors have the Corporate Pass, and that entitles us to a free personal trainer session a week. And I've been with them for more than 10 years now. I joined when I was in Milan, and that's a clear indicator of my loyalty. Surely, they ought to take that into consideration. Maybe I should change gyms or set up a false account and give them bad reviews on TripAdvisor! It's sixty euros for a lesson with Daniele! There's no way I'm paying that. And it's out of my way to get there... No, Francesca, stop that now, you're out of control again! It's worth every minute. Their Rose Pink Himalayan Salt Crystal Bath healed my psoriasis patch, after all. And no one else in town has got one of those! What's more, all my male peers take advantage our weekday free sauna and gym offer at our hotel. Just imagine getting all hot and sticky in the steam bath with Benito the Psycho, Stewed Mutton and friends. I should thank God for small mercies.

***

Twenty-two

And thank God for Angelo. There are two reasons I go to him. The first is that he's the best hairdresser in town, and I don't mind paying extra for that. Nobody has my hair colour. He nails it every time! And the second is that he helps me wind down for the weekend. I mean he's not only witty, he's truly uplifting. He educates me. He's got a gift. He's one of my sprit friends.

We were having coffee between fixing my finger and my roots refurb and he was telling about how the gay community had lobbied so hard for gay rights since Stonewall in 1969, and it had taken nearly 50 years to get gay marriage on the civil registers in Italy. He's not a political activist but he knows his stuff. And then he said that, of course the gay community might look all Tinseltown and Glam when it came to getting married, but taking the vows was deeply meaningful for them, more so than the hetero community in his view, because it wasn't loaded with all the expectations of the hetero world. Well that was a bit opinionated of him, and he's often fooled by his own romanticism, but then he blew me away by saying that heterosexual opposition to gay marriage was based on the conservative heteros' fear of their own promiscuity; in other words projection. *Chapeau!* He told me that the levels of promiscuity between heteros and gays basically evened out thanks to on-line chat rooms. Gays were first off the mark but the breeder community had caught up pretty quickly, and what's more, we breeders were much more decisive and result-oriented when it came to eating our nookie pie. "So, it's Wham bam thank you Ma'am for the heteros, while gays are frequently foiled by the full frontal confrontation before their wardrobe mirrors, and they often prefer to cream the drippy tube while drooling over their webcams, rather than risk a tête-à-tête with a complete stranger". Then the gay community had had its epiphany with the AIDS epidemic of course, with 15 years of unremitting deaths and suffering worldwide before treatments became widely available that made HIV/AIDS survivable. Inevitably, their identity had come a long way from self-hating sluts of the seventies, to the bum-chum promiscuity of the new millennium, and now they're purely polyamorous. Immense pain and suffering had been a horrendous wake up call for them. The promiscuous hetero scene *au contraire* hadn't really got an identity, and were pretty much either all bunny-hopping or fantasizing about it. We had done basically nothing to get over our post-modern Catholic guilt complex, apart from sealing the sleaze in a code of secrecy, hypocrisy and silence. Gays were more self-accepting. Anyway, since 2018, sexually transmitted HIV infections among breeders had overtaken gays, 41% to 39% and nobody talked about it. Now that is shocking! But it's convenient for the God-squaddies to land the "licentious" label on the queer, the quaint and the quirky, while they're flashing their cassocks at Mary Magdalene. And of the heterosexual infections, 23% were male and only 18% female. "Think about that" he said. "It means there are a whole lot of homoblivious women out there, and I wouldn't like to be one of them". He's got a point. Maria-Cristina and Terenzio broke up after being married for nearly twenty-five years. She said she was fed up with being a mother to him and his children, and she dumped him. Pity she missed out on the silver wedding celebrations though. They were planning a cruise in the Caribbean. Anyway, within six months he and Carlo had moved in together. And Carlo's fifteen years younger than Terenzio! Maria-Cristina says she gets on with Carlo like a house on fire. It's incredible really. But it happens so often these days. He also said I was a demi-sapio-sexual, which just about sounds better than a gerontophile. But Edoardo is not that much older than me! Twelve or thirteen years? It's funny how time flies, I can't remember. Oh, look there's Giorgio.

***

Twenty-three

-"Ok darling, sports bag in the boot, and take a seat in the back. What are you eating?"
-It's chewing gum, mum. Tom gave it me. Can't I sit in the front?
-Well, spit it out in the street right now. I don't want that disgusting stuff getting stuck on my upholstered leather seats. The last time you had chewing gum in the car, you disposed of it in the ashtray unbeknown to me, which is where I keep my veneer Gautama Buddha. You know how much it means to me. He was made from Gigi Buffon's tooth caps, which is a great incentive for reincarnation. It took me a whole bottle of Amuchina gel

to clean him up, and that's why I had to miss the first half of your cup final last year.
-Does that mean that Buffon saw me playing in the final?
-You never know, maybe he was there in spirit!
-Well can I sit in the front then?
-Get in but be quick, I've still got to get the bread from the bakery. Your father messed up again.
-Mum, can I have the soft white bread rolls? All the seeds from the organic wholegrain get stuck under my dental braces.
-But the white bread's full of gluten and it will give you tummy ache.
-But I don't like brown bread.
- No buts, I spend all my life running around for you, all your training sessions and matches, and now you're arguing with me over bread!
-I'm not eating it if it's brown.
-Look, I'll pick the seeds out for you. You're not having white bread, it's common. And mama knows best."

***

Twenty-four

Oh, what a Friday. Thank God it's not Friday the 13th, otherwise my husband would be waking up to a suicide note tomorrow morning. I dropped all that TGIF crap years ago, because there's just no time to go out and have an aperitif with my lady friends on Fridays these days. It's Murphy's law. You only have to think TGIF, and it lands you in the shit big time. Not only did the shit hit the fan today, but I was in the muck-spreader fermenting with it. If only those water sprinklers had worked, I wouldn't be in this mess now. Well, that's another lesson learnt. Never trust your male peers to get the job done. They're more likely to bury their head in the sand, or worse still, disappear completely. I've no time for them, they just don't take responsibility for their own actions. They'll never grow up. Then, I managed to make myself an enemy with Benito, whom I get on with best in the entire company. Of course, Benito and I don't see eye-to-eye when it comes to politics; in fact we're not even on the same spectrum. But he's got common sense and a sense of humour, and that's saying something these days with all that corporate drudgery. But I could still risk my job over this… But hang on, didn't I give Anna the task of chasing up Mutton over the sprinklers before she was moved to the hotel? And, she never got back to me on it. Surely, she has to take some of the blame for that. I must have it written in an email somewhere. I do everything in writing with my subordinates… I'll check that tomorrow first thing…. And then, I tore my nail and that was bloody painful. And Daniele wants me to pay for the lesson I missed too. But worst of all, Giorgino! And Stormtrooper is turning him a homophobe. Then there was his maths homework and his stomach ache again, and after we'd fought over the bread, he flatly refused to eat his dinner, went into his room with his Playstation and I haven't seen him since. His light should have been out at 9.30. He's definitely growing up, I know. He answers back all the time. And half the time, he doesn't even want mama to hug him, and he prefers to watch football on TV with his papa. And then there's his sweetheart, Elisa. She reminds me of myself! But how am I going to cope? I'm not ready for him to grow up…..

***

Part two

Growing Pains

One

The Winds of Change - by Dr. Ed Case

Newton befell the apple
And claimed his noble truth.
Inevitably, inexorably, irrefutably,
It stole us of our youth.

And when Eurus chilled the summer
That sweetened many a fruit -
Over the grapes, grain and gourds
All birds and bees fell mute.

And time rolled on with gravity,
With Boreas beating down,
On our lives, our loves, our labours
He cast a sullen frown.

As the days drew close
Harrowing nights grew long
Yet Irreverence, insolence and impertinence
Echoed in the harmonies of your song

Then Zephyr warmed his breath anew
As boughs and meadows greened,
Your home, your hopes, your heart.

Are soon to be redeemed

Your time is far from over
The battle has just begun.
So seek, strive and struggle forth
For the day will still be won!

As the phoenix fans his feathers
And Notus soars o'er skies
By wonder, will and wisdom
You'll claim your cherished prize.

"Dear Ed,

Your poem has been shortlisted for The Four Humours Prize for Poetry and Medicine 2021 open to health professionals in Italy, in the Healing Power of Poetry Section, which will be published in the Four Humours Poetry Anthology 2021.

It is with great pleasure that we invite to attend the Annual Prize-Giving Ceremony at the Gala Dinner for the 10th Italian Poetry and Medicine Symposium in Ancona on 14-15th May. Invited poets may read their own competition entries or a poem of their choice that embodies the spirit of our motto, "Life's worth Living", and say why this poem means so much to him/her. The dinner will take place on Friday evening, and on Saturday, we have planned an organised tour of the Marches, which will include a visit to the home of our great lyric poet Giacomo Leopardi.

Full details of the programme of events are attached, together with enrolment forms. Please confirm your booking by return to the following email address, and not later than, 14th March 2021: info@fourhumourspoetry.it

The 2021 Prize Anthology is available to order by PayPal or direct bank transfer from our website at www.fourhumours-poetry.org.

Looking forward to your reply……"

Well how about that. The letter that 's poised to change my destiny! Sleepless nights and creativity is paying off after all. We all get bored on night shifts, and some of them are interminable. Renato chats and watches porno videos when he's feeling restless, or that's what he says at any rate. But we've all heard him snoring like a flatulent hippo stuck down a waterhole on many an occasion! A weekend in Ancona eh? Ah, that fresh sea breeze, and I could take a spin down to the Conero. Franci and I used to love our weekend getaways to the *Conchiglia Verde* in Sirolo when we were young at heart. Perhaps she'll be up for it again. The poetry symposium is just a bit of a lark, and we haven't had a weekend away this year. See what she says. Of course, I'd never read that poem in public. It's dreadful. I've got no illusions about that. Good job I used a *nom de plume*. I'd be really ashamed if any of my

colleagues got wind of this! They're merciless. I only did it to alleviate the boredom.
I'll try giving her a call. She's not home. I never see her.

-"Traumschwarz, I thought we might at least have breakfast together, this morning. Where are you?
-I had to dash off early to Gemma's. She's my nail technician.
-Ah, right, and when are you back?
-Listen, as I'm already out of the house, I thought I'd do the weekly shop. I've left you a note in the kitchen. It says: "get Giorgio his breakfast, switch on the washing machine, Setting No. 5 for the shirt wash at 90°". I didn't want to wake Giorgio. He always has a lie in on Saturdays. If he's not up before ten, wake him. Then, get his breakfast. He wouldn't have dinner last night so he should be really hungry. But not Coco Pops, he had those yesterday. I've got some sugar-free organic muesli with blackcurrant and marigold-flavoured Skyr that needs finishing in the fridge. He likes that. Then you two can go down to the park for a couple of hours. You can take him skateboarding. It's a lovely day. I'll be back at midday, then we can have some pasta for lunch. Afternoon is free time until 4.30pm. I'm going shopping with Chiara. Then Giorgio is having a sleepover at Thomas' again. So if you could take him over there too, I can get ready to go out later. Chiara's invited us over for drinks, so we might end up having dinner there together, or going to a restaurant. That's just about everything. How does that sound? Oh, and by the way, if you're back before me at 12, don't

forget to put the washing out on the clothes stand. And don't make a mess. It took me an hour to clean up after you yesterday. It looked Hannibal and the Elephants had been having a picnic in the kitchen.
-Right, got it.
-So why did you call?
-Errm can't remember. Don't worry, I'm sure my amnesia will be over by lunchtime. See you later Traumschwarz!

❋❋❋

Two

-"Papa, what time is it?
- Morning Giorgio. Almost ten. What would you like for breakfast? Coco Pops is it?
-Are you sure? Great! I love Coco Pops.
-So what's the problem?
-Well nothing really, but mum doesn't usually let me have them two days running. She says they're full of sugar and that if I'm not careful I'll be diabetic by the time I'm a teenager.
-Nonsense. Is she a bit stressed again? But if you don't want Coco Pops, you can always have the organic muesli and skyr. You know that thick clotted white amalgam the Vikings gorge on before they go off culling whales, dolphins and seals!
-Do they really? Wow!

-No, it's just a joke. Your papa is getting a bit sarcastic in his old age. So what's it to be, Coco Pops or muesli?
-I'll have Cocoa Krispies, thanks. That's what they're called in England, papa.
-You're a smarty pants, aren't you?
-And can I have an extra big portion? I didn't have any dinner last night. I had a fight with mama and went to my room. She said I couldn't come out until I said sorry.
-And?
-I didn't say sorry, so I stayed in my room.
-That'll teach you. Well then, you can finish the packet off if you like. There's not that much in there anyway.
-You're fighting a lot with your mum at the moment. What's the problem?
-Well she treats me like I'm a baby, and she's really bossy.
-Come on Giorgio, she does everything for you. That's what mums are like. They'll do anything for you but you have to give them a lot of hugs in return, okay. And when you get to my age, it's much better if you exchange the hugs for your credit card, otherwise they get the strops! Got it?
-Okay, ….but are you coming to see my match tomorrow?
-Next week, yes. Tomorrow I've got to work all day at A&E in the hospital. I'm on call. Your mum's going to be there isn't she?
-Yes, but that's not the same. She gets really crazy when someone fouls me. She nearly had a fight with one of the mum's from the away team last week.

-Guess she's a bit feisty. She's really passionate about you winning. She's your number one fan.
-Well I call it embarrassing. She got so mad that she said that black kids shouldn't be playing in our league. Only she didn't say black, she used the "N" word.
-Did she now? That is interesting…You've got to learn to be patient with her, she means well.
-Dad, can I ask you a question?
-Go on then. Well it's something Tom said.
-Okay (….*I've got a feeling I know what's coming…*).
-Is it true that gays and mums suck dicks?
-Hmm… Tom is a lively kid, isn't he?
-Are you angry with me for asking?
-No, no, you're just getting to that curious age aren't you? Listen, adults do all sorts of strange things with each others' bodies. But most of the time, it's just grown-ups playing. You don't need to worry about it. Really, it's nothing at all.
-So should me and Elisa do that too? I don't want her to suck my willy.
-Well that's a relief..I mean you drink coca-cola, and have ice-cream together, and..?
-..we text each other, and last week she let me kiss her on the lips.
-Well that's all you need to be doing for now. Right, it's time we were going to the park young man. Have you got your skateboard?
-Yep!
-Let's be off then.

※※※

Three

-"ST. It's me. Where are you?

-We're just on our way back from the park. Five minutes, and we'll be home.

-But it's nearly half-past. I said twelve. And there's an empty Coco Pops packet in the plastics section of the separate waste collection bin. Giorgio was supposed to have the muesli. You defied me again!

-Oh Franci, come on, you know I'm colour-blind, I always get the wrong bin.

-That's not funny. I've just about had enough of being mother to an inept and dishonest fifty-six year old child.

-But Giorgio is just a boy, and it's Saturday morning. Chill out. What's stressing you so much? By the way, Giorgio came off his skateboard, and grazed his knee. He's a bit sore but he'll be alright. He's handled the pain really well, and I didn't have to counsel him. He's a tough guy!

-What are you going on about? Counselling? Is he okay? Put him on to me now. I need to speak to him.

-Here he is...

-Mama...

-Giorgino, are you okay, really? Papa is so irresponsible.

-Papa's winding you up again, I'm fine, really.. I've just got a bit of a bruise on my left knee.

-Well it's your cup match next week, and I don't want you to miss that.

-No way!
-Well, put him back on to me.
-Ok mama.
-See, he's okay, just having a bit of fun.
-Well, we'll see who gets the last laugh! I've put all the shopping away, and there's the washing to hang out. I'm not cooking. I'm cream crackered so you can take us out to lunch.
-You've certainly got a way with words Franci, where do you want to go?
-I don't care, you decide.
-Giorgio's asking if we can go to have a Big Mac? He's says it's more than a year since you let him have one.
-Get serious, or you'll be having a reverse puberty operation before you're through the door, Dr. Cassese! And in the afternoon, I'm out shopping for my annual conference outfit with Chiara. So we've only got about an hour for lunch.
-It's definitely a No Mac, Giorgio! Don't worry, I promise you'll have something you like. But seriously Franci, when is your annual conference?
-Last year it was postponed because of the takeover, so now it's in May.
-Not the third weekend?
-That's it, you guessed right again, 14-16th May. Are you a clairvoyant?
-Well, it's just that I've been shortlisted for a poetry prize… and… No, no forget that. I didn't say anything.

-What's that Stormtrooper? Your creative juices are flowing again? It's been more than a decade…You never said anything. I want to know all about that…
-No forget it, Franci, it doesn't matter. I probably won't be able to get the time off anyway.
-Come on Edo. I'm not backing down on this.
- Vergißt - Vergaß – Vergessen! Just revising my irregular verb tables. I'm hanging up now. We're outside the door.

***

Four

-"Chiara, it's me. I'm ten minutes late…
-Franci, well that's okay, I'm flirting with the waiter at the bar. He's super handsome - a really puppy look to him. I wonder if he's got that biscuit breath that all little puppy dogs have?
-Chiara, how many spritz have you downed? Sometimes I worry about you, really I do.
-I'm just squishing the slice of orange at the bottom of my first glass; if you get a move on I'll wait to have the second with you. So what are we shopping for today, Madam Lash? Are we doing sex toys, lingerie or latex? If it's toys you're after, Hot Breath do a great line in dicks for dykes!
-Chiaraaaaa, stop!
-No but seriously, Edo's is in the same queue as Rocco Siffredi when it comes to having his prostate checked, so he should be well due for his digital rectal exam by now. I

think a strap-on might be just up his street after all. And you could certainly give him more than he's bargaining for on April Fool's.

-The bargain, my dear Chiara, is that this shop is out of business! I don't do sex toys, got it? You are completely mad anyway – and obsessed! We're going to get my evening dinner dress for the annual conference. It's black tie optional so that's definitely below the knee but I'm not doing a full-length; light and sky blues are back in again this year. I've seen something I want your second opinion on in Luisa Spagnoli.

- You're not going as Elsa in Frozen again, are you? Frost maidens packed their suitcases with the melting of the Last Ice Age!

-Come on Chiara. It's my favourite colour and you know it suits me. I've got all the accessories and shoes to match already, and I don't want to fork out a fortune this year.

-I reserve judgment. Where are you? I'm gagging for another spritz.

-I'm standing right in front of you.

❋❋❋

Five

…-"Hi Sanjeet Kaur, you don't usually ring me on a Sunday morning? Everything okay?... Oh dear, not your cat? Yes, I know he'd been ill for a while, and he hadn't had much of an appetite. .. He hadn't been eating for how long ? What nearly two weeks? That's terrible. But didn't the vet do the tests, and they came back negative? …So, how old was he?… Fourteen, oh poor old Simba Mafusa, and he was just like the Lion King, with his ginger fur and his funny sticky-out ears. Are you going to cremate him? …I see, you can't do that before Monday, and no, I didn't know that they do a communal cremation for pets and then just share out the ashes… No, no of course not, I wouldn't want to spend the rest of my life looking at my neighbour's dog in an urn on my bed chest, either… Look, I really am sorry. If there's anything I can do to help? Listen, have you thought about doing a burial? … Yes, there is pet cemetery just out of town. You can choose the tombstone and write an epitaph. And you get to put a photo on the tombstone. They even do a funeral service. I took Gemma once to lay flowers at Josie's tombstone… You know her cockapoo, Josie, the one that got electrocuted at the dog groomers. And she goes back there every month. She says it's very restful. And every Friday, they hold a remembrance service for anyone who's interested. There's always a good turnout. They've got all sorts of pets there. It's a sort of ghost zoo. Apart from dogs, there are cats and rabbits of course, but there are also hamsters, guinea pigs, turtles, terrapins, cockatoos and budgies, and I even saw one for a goldfish called Jaws! ….Yes, I agree, it really is sad and it will be hard for you, and you're on your own now…. What's that? Well no…actually, no I can't, I'm sorry, I can't come over right now, I promised Giorgino I'd take him to Mass. How about if we have a coffee together before the class tomorrow evening? I'd like that. …We were just about through the door when you rang... Yesterday, Chiara and I decided that it was high time Giorgino and Thomas had a spiritual education. …Yes, I do know you do a meditation course for kids… We can think about that…Well, the two of them are getting just a bit too curious about "sexual organs" and that sort of thing; Giorgio's obsessed about me and gays doing fellatio. And now that the Church has cleaned up its act on pedophilia, we thought it was high time.. No, of course I don't give gays blow jobs. What are you talking about? You've got the wrong end of the stick, there! Listen, we've really got to dash. I'll call you tomorrow. And I'm so, so sorry.

❋❋❋

Six

-"Aunt Dot. You just caught me just in time. I was about to board the docking station and launch an arse rocket. And you know what, I've always wanted to be an astronaut.

-Of course the phone's in the socket, otherwise I wouldn't be able to speak to you. And what's that about you wanting to see a man about a horse? Be quick, dear nephew, or you'll burn your brownies! But just let me take my hearing aid out. There's a lot of interference and I can't hear you properly.

-Well, how have you been keeping Dot?

-Not so bad, I suppose.

-Well you don't sound all that plucky.

-Well I'm not. You know my knee is still no better, so I just can't go out.
-Well, is it any worse?
-Not really. I'm just a bit depressed. I've always been so active. And to have to rest up like this.
-Well, did you go back to your old medicine in the end?
-No, not in the end. I just upped the dose.
-And the bulkiness?
-Well, no that's righted itself, so maybe it wasn't the new medicine after all. Or it just took a few days of getting used to.
-Well that's good news. Perhaps in a couple of days, the pain will start to ease too.
-I'll just have to get used to being ninety and putting up with the pain. Anyway I've decided I'm going to cook a proper lunch today. Roland bought me some salmon from Waitrose. He's a lovely man. He always pops round to see if there's anything I need.
-And he does your weekly shop.
-Yes he does. I don't know what I'd do without him.
-Well, have you thought any more about getting home help in the daytime? You know, just to have someone round and a regular basis. Maybe just the mornings, to help you get started?
-No, no. I've got Agneska, who comes in one morning a week to do the cleaning. That's enough, really it is.
-Well, I was just thinking that maybe, if you had someone in to help you get washed and dressed, you'd feel a little bit more on top of things, and it would give you some company.

-Well, I'm not handicapped, you know. Now that the bulkiness has stopped, I only have to empty the colostomy bag twice a day, which I can cope with. Before it was a nightmare.
-I guess you're very proud.
-Well I am, yes.
-So how is your garden then?
-Well, you know it's rained a lot lately.
-Yeh?
-Since we last spoke, I decided to walk 10 lengths of the garden each morning, and last week the laburnum had just started to put out its leaves. So, this morning, after another night's rain, all its flower chains were hanging down, ready to open. I could have sworn that yesterday they hadn't even sprouted. So I'm quite looking forward to that.
-Yes, your laburnum is exceptional with all its golden yellow flowers. Guess what Aunt Dot, I had an incredible experience yesterday morning, quite out of the ordinary. I was about to make coffee for breakfast and I spotted this beautiful little blackcap just sitting there on the balcony. First, I thought maybe he's injured or shocked or something, and then I thought I'd better move him quick, otherwise the dogs will snaffle him up. They always get a bread roll for breakfast and their pretty impatient. So I went out, and he didn't move. I put my leather gardening gloves on and cupped my hands and he just nestled in. So I popped him in a little wicker basket that I keep some old cloths in. Well, can you imagine, he just wouldn't come unstuck from my glove, so I had to slip it off and

leave it there with the blackcap hanging on. It was quite touching. Maybe, he'd flown into the verandah window or got cold, I just don't know. I was able to look straight into his beady black eyes. Fantastic! Anyway, I just left him there. Of course, when I decided I'd take a photo half an hour later, he wasn't playing anymore and no sooner had I opened the door and he flew up into the trees. And that was that.

-Oh, yes, that *is* marvellous. And how did you know he was a male?

-Well, I checked that out on the internet.

-Yes, because the females only have a brown cap.

-Dot, you know everything about birds. And I discovered that he's one of our most tuneful songbirds too, with an epic repertoire. A top warbler!

-Really, I didn't know that. I can tell a greenfinch from a chaffinch, though. Oh well, that's just gorgeous. Is that the time? My programme's about to start. I'll have to be going, I haven't had my mid-morning decaf coffee yet. Bye darling. That's really cheered my day up.

-Bye Aunt Dot, sending my love…. Oh, she's gone.."

❊❊❊

Seven

-"Mama, why are we going to Mass today? We never go into churches unless it's because you want to see paintings of Jesus, Mary and Saints, or frescoes of biblical stories in the chapels. And you promised you would never make me go to Mass if I finished my catechism classes. And I did.

-This is different. Thomas and Chiara are coming too, and we decided that you boys needed a bit of a spiritual education. You're both developing tastes for things you're not old enough to understand.

-Well I don't understand what spiritual means.

-Giorgio, it means that you have to have firm moral beliefs so that you don't get distracted by things that could harm your growth and development.

-And what does that mean?

-Look, it's like this: we all want to become better people than we are in everyday life, and we all know that our better self exists, so we go to church to listen to a priest who sets us a good example about how to behave by reflecting on the life of Jesus. And then we pray that it can come true. How does that sound?

-Boring. Tom and I arranged a Fornite Challenge and now we're going to miss it.

-Well, there's more to life than Playstation, so you can start by reflecting on that! Pope Francis says that we should follow the example of Jesus in the Gospels and evangelise, "Ask and you will receive, and your joy will be complete".

-Does that mean I can go on my Playstation afterwards?

-Don't be so insolent; I think we're going to need to do a lot of this in future. Jesus said it in his Sermon on the Mount, which you learnt about an your catechism, and what he meant was, that we will all get good things in life if we know how to cultivate what is good. And today's sermon is about that. Oh, look there's Chiara with Tom. Come on".

Don Donato Pasticcio's Homily

"….And this millennium has thrown up many new challenges for our peoples of the Christian faith, the world over. Globalisation has brought many technological improvements for the benefit of humanity, with a 40% reduction in deaths from communicable diseases worldwide in the past 25 years. I'm sure you will all agree that this is remarkable progress. And at the same time, with the digital revolution and the advent of the platform economies, we can have everything at the touch of a button. The pace of life has sped up significantly, opening up a world of opportunity. And perhaps our greatest difficulty today is knowing how and what to choose, so that we can fill our lives with value, and not just worthless objects that stand as an impediment in the way of the Lord, our Saviour.

Pope Francis said that that "fear of change leads us to build up fences and obstacles to the terrain of the common good, turning it into a minefield of hatred and incomprehension". And that brings me back to my main theme of today's sermon, which I have taken from the Gospel of Saint Matthew. In his Sermon on the Mount, Jesus said, and I quote from the New Testament, Matthew, Chapter Seven, verses seven and eight:

> *7. "Ask, and it will be given you. Seek, and you will find. Knock, and it will be opened for you.*
> *8. For everyone who asks receives. He who seeks finds. To him who knocks it will be opened".*

Of course today, we widely consider this passage to be a metaphor for prayer, and when we knock at the door of the God, we to need to know what it is we are asking for. It is only when we ask from the purity or the bottom of our hearts that we can cultivate what it is good. Let's reflect on that: it is only when we ask according to God's will that he will hear our prayers. For if we give God our love, he will return it with love.

Globalisation has also heightened our perceptions of the disparity between the rich and the poor, the developed world and the developing world. And this is leading to demographic pressures with mass migrations pushing up from the South towards our coasts. So now, as your shepherd, I ask you as the Italian people who have congregated here today to pray for a better tomorrow, and I must ask you in all sincerity, if you feel that we can continue accept thousands of immigrants without using our judgment and discernment. Is that the tomorrow you have prayed for from the bottom of your hearts? Surely, if we are to do good in God's name, we cannot welcome immigrants indiscriminately. Imagine a glass that can hold 100ml of water. What if were to attempt to pour 200ml into the glass? It overflows. It's mathematical. And of course, it's our moral duty to help the poor and needy, and many of them are arriving at our shores; yet there are also many who come, not out of fear of persecution, but they arrive with mobile phones wearing gold chains, in search of economic gain. And they will take our jobs from us. And what I say is that there are already too many poor Italians that need our help. So now, as we approach our prayers, let us ask for God's guidance and reassurance, and for our political leaders to find the faith and resilience necessary to protect our borders.

And now let us all stand together to recite the creed...."

-Franci, I'm out of here.
-Me too, that's despicable, he's inciting racial hatred from the bottom of his heart! I've never heard anything like it.
-Outrageous. And all that propaganda about stealing our jobs. I mean last week, there was a band of extortionists who got arrested for making the immigrant labourers work twelve hour days for €3 an hour. And if they said they were tired, they just beat them. One of them lost and eye last week. And they call it working for a cooperative! And the arsehole of a priest has never done a day's work in his life. That's the worst bit. He's a parasite feeding of the charitable ignorance of the whole community. Spiritual guidance indeed, you son of a bitch! At least Pope Francesco was a missionary.
-Okay Chiara, take it easy.
-Come on guys. It's definitely time for a Big Mac.
-Chiara, anything but a Big Mac, please.
-Get off your high horse, Helen of Troy. You dragged me through the city all afternoon yesterday, and today you wanted to make a convert out of me. My moral education days are over. You've certainly boosted my atheist's ego.
-Mama, what's an atheist?
-Giorgino, it's someone who doesn't believe in God.
-Oh wow, I like the sound of that.
-Well, let's keep an open mind, because you're not old enough to be atheist. You're only twelve and a half. At most, you can be an agnostic okay, because they don't know what to believe in.

-Mama, how old do I have to be to become an atheist?

-Franci, these kids don't believe in anything except Fornite and MacDonalds. Their only faith is to be able to have and do what their friends do because that's what we ram down their throats from Day One. You can have this, you can't have that. Do this, don't do that. We just don't give them the space to explore their own needs and feelings. We control them obsessively.

-Chiara, look it's not that simple, I mean..

-Mum?

-Yes Tommi.

-Why did the priest want to pour 200ml of water into a 100ml glass? That's stupid. Nobody would even try to do that. And why do we help immigrants and not Italians?

-No, the priest said we should help Italians and not immigrants, darling!

-Well that's not fair either. Lots of our schoolmates are from immigrant families or have mixed parents and I want to help them too. Last week in our art class, we had to paint a picture called "All in the same Boat". It was really cool, cos' first our teacher let us do drama.

-What do you mean by that?

-Well first, all the Italian children had to stand together, and the others – you know the foreign ones and kids like Elisa who's got a Romanian dad - all linked arms and made the shape of a boat around them. Then we had to imagine crossing an ocean. The Italians had to imagine that they might drown, and the others had to save them. Then Mr. Sartori played this incredible scary classical music as we sailed across the ocean. When we got to the other side of the room we all hugged each other. Then we swapped roles and did it again. We all got really excited about it, and some of us cried. Giorgio did, didn't you Giorgio?

-No I didn't..I have hay fever and my eyes were itchy.

-Anyway, it was brilliant because I hugged some classmates that I don't even usually talk to at school, and it made me feel really good. And it made me think that it's stupid to be horrible to people just because they look different.

-Well, last week my mum said that "niggers" shouldn't be allowed to play on the football team.

-Franci! You didn't?

-Well, I didn't mean it. It just slipped out because one of them fouled Giorgino really badly when he was about to score a goal. You know me. I know I shouldn't have said it. Anyway, I won't do it again. It really was bad, and totally out of character.

-Nobody's perfect, Franci. But I suggest you go and confess with Don Pasticcio next week. The two of you seem to be one the same wavelength!

-Giorgio, do you remember what the music was?

-I think he said it was Desiree singing with Verdi and Eminem, or something, but it was the first time I'd heard it!

-No, sweet, I think perhaps it was *Dies Irae* from Verdi's Requiem!

-Is that Latin mama?

-Yes darling, and it means Day of Wrath!

❋❋❋

Eight

-"Mr. Con…sorry, Jeff. This is an early call for Monday, I'm on my way in to work, to what do I owe this honour?
-Hi Francesca. Bad news I'm afraid. Mutton is going to be off for a month; he's clinically depressed. Not the best start to the week, given the circumstances. And that puts me in a bit of a corner. I was wondering, do you think you handle the reporting to our superiors and with the public authorities on Mutton's behalf in the intervening period?
-Yep, can do that. We need to make sure his team know about it. The maintenance guys are the worst when it comes to insubordination with women. And it would be a good idea if they took down their Biker Babe Calendars from the notice board next to the drinks vending machine for the time being too.
-Don't worry, I'll sort that.
-To be frank, I feel much better about managing this myself than depending on Mutton. … Listen, I spoke to the Chief of the Fire Service and the week end, and we decided that we should move in the following way: first, we report that the cause of the fire was due to the cleaner negligently leaving the chemical cleaning agent on the hob, which he accidentally switched on during cleaning.
-What the cleaner was a man?
-Do you really think a woman would be so inadvertent?

-Suppose you're right there.

-In fact, this whole botch job is a 100% male-dominated show and I'm being sexist when I say that. Mutton failing to service the sprinklers or get the certification; the clumsy cleaner, and Popeye the security guard puffing on his old pipe!

-I get it Francesca, but what about the water sprinklers?

-Then, and this is the good part, we have to say that the fire caused a general power failure, and the circuit breakers deactivated the entire mainframe, which is why the sprinklers weren't activated. And the Fire Chief will corroborate that. Listen, we're going to need to dip into the Reserve Fund for this, but we can talk about this when we're face to face.

-Got you.

-Jeff, can I miss the team meeting? I've got a lot on my plate this morning, what with the Damage Loss Consultant and stepping in for Mutton.

Yes, I'll apologise to the other team members on your behalf.

-Let's do a catch up call before lunch. Remember, we also need to keep our focus on our own internal damage assessment so that we can estimate how long it will be before the restaurant can reopen.

-Another thing, Jeff.

-What's that Francesca?

-Well maybe this is an ideal opportunity to rename the restaurant. As we've said on several occasions, we're the laughing stock with the local tourist trade, since we chose the name Matka. Having a restaurant called "The Uterus" in Russian is hardly a crowd-puller. It's been a long-standing joke with the Russians guests for the past two years, and those smart Sashas are always asking us for vagina-key-ring souvenirs.

-Well, yes, I shall certainly give that some thought to that too.

-What the souvenirs?

- I certainly know where I'd like to stuff their sturgeons! Bye Francesca.

-That's funny. Good alliteration Jeff !"

※※※

Nine

Well it's all going to plan. Francesca you are a genius. You've still got to make up with Benito. That might be a tough one, but knowing him, he'll just act as though nothing happened last week. Men are like that. They are terrified of their own emotions. They never want to show their anger at work, so when they do, afterwards they cocoon themselves in their chrysalis of shame. It's a question of honour for them. They pride themselves on being one of the boys, able to play the game at all costs. They wind each other with pungent sarcasm, and even offend one another. But as long as they're all on a level playing field, they become artful masters at ducking the blows. I mean last week, Benito was winding Stewart up something rotten about not being able to see his kids since his ex-wife had petitioned for custody of the children. Of course, Stewart took the bait and – full of bravado – retaliated bragging that now he was a free man, he was looking forward to dining out with his colleagues' wives while they were away on business. While the cat's away, the mice will play sort of thing. Of course, I would have gone for the jugular - if their wives hadn't already divorced them, it wasn't to due to the sexual prowess, it simply meant they'd already found alternative sources of amusement and even better ways of emptying their loving hubbies' credit cards….The best place to strike is never below the belt, but in their pockets! And that's why it's so hard to deal with me. I play a different ball game. So with me they're on tenterhooks all the time. That's the way they are. Birds of a feather flock together. Only now, Stewart will be off work depressed for at least a month! That all goes to show just how resilient men are, doesn't it? Anyway, the important thing is that Benito doesn't brood on my insults for too long, otherwise he'll get morose licking his wounds; that's dangerous, because that's when men regress into that sulky childhood state and it can go on for weeks. Just like you've deprived them of their favourite toys. Oh look, surprise, surprise, he's calling me now.

"Hi Benito... Franci here… Yes, I've got time for a quick chat. How have you been?.. Yeh, me too, had quite a fun weekend, actually. Even got to see Don Pasticcio's performance live. .. Yes, I know it's all over the local paper, even on the national radio this morning. We walked out. Well, it was disgraceful, not even you'd take it that far. …Oh come on, no need to apologise. Forget about it, sticks and stones will break my bones….. We were all a bit stressed a the end of last week, what with the fire incident. ..yeh, that would be great. Let's have a spritz or something! At the moment, I'm pretty free. ..Well if I don't see you in the canteen, I'll see you tonight at our usual place. Six-thirty? …Great…. Oh what's that sorry? Did I hear you correctly? What…? Anna has handed in her notice at the hotel? No, she can't have. She wouldn't. Jesus, this spells trouble!

※※※

Ten

It's only been a weekend since I saw Lemon Tart, and I'm starting to get a bit jumpy. I don't want to give the impression that I'm too keen, but at the same time, it was definitely something special, and I haven't felt like that for …I can't even remember how long. I mean wow – it certainly got my yoghurt cannon curdling…I've been practicing a few new expressions too…. and I'm definitely up for another poke at the squid. There's a lot of that terminology on the internet. It'll take a lifetime to learn it all. Well maybe I should just send a quick "ciao" to say hello and that I'm interested in doing a remake of the epic battle with Darth Vader. And it's my day off on Wednesday, so we wouldn't have to rush things like last time. And that's plenty of notice. Right let's do it. See what happens. The next time we can exchange numbers. I can get a second SIM card.

"Hey!.."

There's a green light to show that Lemon Tart is on line, but no answer. I'll check later, after lunch.

***

Eleven

-"So Mr. Ciullo, that's not a local name is it?
-No, you're right, it's an Apulian surname. My parents were originally from Lecce, but please call me Beato. Apparently, my surname comes from the archaic word for child, *fanciullo*, which in turn originated in Tuscany. Nothing to do with its slang meaning in the north of Italy, of course.
-So, it's *Beato Ciullo*?
-Yes, that raises quite a few eyebrows, but I'm used it, don't worry, I've got a hard shell.
-Beato, what would you like to choose from the menu?
-So, Mrs Scarpa, is yours a local name too? I think I'm just going to have a main course. I like to eat light at

lunch. Maybe the sea bass for me with some cooked veg. How about you?

-Ha! my name was also a source of derision at school too, I can tell you, and yes, it's a local name. Franny Boots was my nickname, and that used to really annoy me. Anyway, I've got quite a sharp tongue and I've always been able to defend myuself. The roast sea bass with that delicate champagne and yuzu miso sauce does sounds irresistible. But call me Franci, please. Listen, I'm really not that hungry. I was dreading the inspection this morning. I've just got no appetite. But if you insist, I'll just have the Cantabrian anchovy and cuttlefish salad.

-Oh Francesca, Franci that's too modest of you. I bet you're a real foodie deep down.

-Well, I have my moments, but I've got the annual conference and gala dinner coming up, and I promised myself I would be in top form for that.

-Ok, I won't push you, but only if you agree to cork a bottle of white wine with me. And you have to choose it too. You're the local expert here.

-Well, I never drink at lunch because against company policy, which I implemented, of course, but this is an exceptional occasion, and rules are made to be broken. But only one glass.

-So what do you suggest?

-Well, I'd go for a *Garda Colli Mantovani Doc*. It's a peculiar local white wine made from a blend of grapes. I can't remember them all, but I know it's got autochthonous Garganega and Trebbiano di Soave grapes, and I think it might have some Chardonnay or

Riesling or something. They stock *Terre di Olfino* here, and it's a fresh dry white with a rich floral bouquet. I think you'll like it with the sea bass.

-My God, you've blown me a way. You must be a Master sommelier, at least!

-No, of course not.. My husband loves his wine, I usually do the buying in, so it's rubbed off on me too.

-Oh, by the way, you needn't worry about the assessment, the inspection went really well. I just need to check a couple of things with the Chief of the Fire Service. And I should be able to get a report to you by the middle of the week.

-Well, that's a relief…. Just a second that's my phone. Would you mind? It's my yoga instructor. I promised to see her later today, but there's no way I can fit it in. I'd better answer.

-Be my guest.

-Sanjeet, I mean Wanda, ….no, it's not a bad time. Really, it's wonderful to hear from you. ..Yes, I remember, we did say that we'd go for a coffee before tonight's Kundalini-Biking session to the summit of Everest. I'd love to yes… but, unfortunately, we're in crisis management at work, it's crazy here. The Maintenance Director is ill so I'm doing two jobs. Really, it's awful, there was a fire in the hotel restaurant kitchen last week, and we had the insurance damage assessment all morning, and then our own team has to evaluate what to do next. I'm with the damage assessor now… So how's your cat? …Sorry, I mean how are you? How stupid of me, I'm getting all mixed up and my words aren't matching my thoughts. I'm in a such a spin…. What's that? What

do you mean it's a sign, Sanjeet?...Yes, well I know that kundalini means coiled snake in Sanskrit, and? ...okay, yeh, I'm with you, the spiritual awakening is also known as the Serpentine Fire as the snake uncoils and releases its divine power.. which many believe to be a divine feminine energy force? And.... So what does that mean? ...We had a fire in the hotel restaurant kitchen!... Yes, there was an explosion, actually...What's that? Is there a sink next to the cooker? Well, as a matter of fact, yes there is.... What? Kitchens are symbols of wealth and prosperity... but according to Feng Shui, cookers and sinks should not be placed next to each other... Sanjeet, sorry if I'm interrupting, and this is incredibly interesting, but I haven't got a clue where it's all leading...In a nutshell? ...What do you mean, it's a warning sign?...Fire can symbolize the destructive forces of human emotions, and you can sense there's a highly powerful female energy force about to erupt in my life and bring disharmony into my marriage...Oh my God, stop there, please, Sanjeet. Look, it's not my kitchen, anyway... Yes, I know I agreed to take responsibility for it, but that's hardly relevant, it's just my job....And no, I can't light red candles and paint pink triangles in the hotel kitchen. This is not the Gay Pride Headquarters. We've got to reopen for Easter. Look, it's a nightmare..... What's that, anger, frustration, impulsiveness and anxiety in my life are related to excessive fire energy?... Wanda have you gone completely crazy?... So how do I rebalance it then? ..By opening myself to compassion?.. Look, I'll definitely find time for coffee this week. Thanks for all your insights and advice. ...Bye then.

-I'm sorry about that. It's a long story...

-She's rather intense I must say. My wife was a yoga teacher too, just the same. But she did Hatha Yoga. She said it was relaxing, but I wouldn't know. That was a few years back. I like to eat well and have a couple of drinks and burn it all off cycling at the weekend. By the way, you're in great shape, Franci. My compliments. Anyway, I did first level reiki at a weekend course once, while I was having one of my mystic moments. I was really into all that energy-healing stuff several years ago. It was called the Mount Kurama Academy and the teacher's claimed their technique descended directly from its founder…
Mikao Usui!
-Wow, you know that too..I'm so impressed Franci, really. Are you the first ever Grand Master Reiki-Sommelier?
-No way, come off it. I owe it all to Sanjeet, or Wanda to her friends. She claims to have done every holistic healing course under the sun. And she's probably right too. But I've always been fascinated by Reiki, and would like to take it up. ..Ah here's the waiter, time to order…

………

-…Well really, I'm so impressed with you Beato! I mean, I just don't how you fit in Voluntary Ambulance Driving for the 118 Emergency Service, and a full-time job. I mean working nights must be terrible. How do you catch up with your sleep?
-Been doing it a long time. That's an old story too.
-I know it's a bit cheap of me to ask, but how do you cope with all the drama and tragedy? It must be

horrendous. All my safety work is based on planning, procedures, and prevention. We call it the three P's. This fire thing was the first serious incident in my career.

-Well, let's say we just try to focus on being there to help people who are in need. They're desperate and beside themselves if they're conscious. If they're not, we try to focus on saving their lives. It's quite a simple formula really. It can be very hard, but also very rewarding.

-Here's the waiter again. Please can you put that on the company account. Thank you very much.

-Well thank you Francesca, I wasn't expecting that, and it really wasn't necessary. You've been a perfect host. Listen, can I give you my card? It's been a real pleasure meeting you. Maybe, if I'm in the area, I could give you a call and we could perhaps go out for a drink. No strings attached!

-Yes' let's… I'd love that. Here's my card too. Oh, I was forgetting, Beato. We spent all lunch talking about ourselves, I had been meaning to ask if you have any children. I've got a son, Giorgio; he's about to become a teenager, and he's definitely got growing pains.

-I did have, yes. They were my growing pains, but that's another story. Oh is that the time? Listen, I really have to dash, I was supposed to be at another company in Brescia half an hour ago. I'll call them.

-Me too, half past three. It's really late for me too. The time has just flown by. Thanks again. I look forward to receiving your report, and who knows, see you again soon.

-You too Francesca, great company, great lunch; sometimes you feel more at ease with total strangers than with your closest friends.

※※※

Twelve

Let's check the Internet. No sign of Lemon Tart. I could try sending another message, I suppose. Maybe the first one didn't get through….

"Hey, Fiore, how are you? Get in touch. Wednesday is my day off. Stormtrooper!"

Thinking about it, sending that second message was definitely not a good idea. It made me look weak and lonely. And desperate! And I'm not any of those, objectively speaking. I've a successful career, I'm a respected married man, with an above average quality of life. So what am I doing here? …This is not for me, I knew it. I should just cancel my nick and eliminate my account, end of story. In fact, Yes, I'll do it now… But Christ, this is complicated, I've never been a wiz kid, I've got reasonable computer skills but this is proving just too difficult…It seems impossible to cancel. This is definitely the first time in my life that regret having developed nerd immunity. …. Ah, what's this? Here, we are…. Oh, and what's this popup now?

"Oh no, are you really sure you want to cancel your account?
You'll lose all your personal photos and messages.
Why not try our free trial Plus membership for two months?"
Click here!

No, I don't want to lose those photos of Lemon Tart. Not now. I even get a hard on just looking at them. Let's give it a bit longer. There are lots of rational explanations for this. I'm definitely being too impulsive here. At my age, I should have a little more patience, and self-respect, and above all, self-control. But this chat thing. It's really got a hold on me. It's the promise of more of what I haven't got in my life. I must be mad.

※※※

Thirteen

Now that's strange. Chiara always answers. Her phone's not off or engaged. I've been trying to call her all afternoon. I'd better text her. I've just got to tell her about lunch.

"Chiara, where are you? Call me asap!"

Where are your friends when you need them most. Mobile phones have got a lot to answer for. Just imagine if my grandmother had met someone she really liked and she'd wanted to tell her best friend about it. She'd have probably written a poem or painted a watercolour or something and then sent it by post. If the horse-drawn carriages didn't get stuck in the mud, and survived the surprise forays of Robin Hood and his Merry Men, it might have arrived after a couple of weeks, by which time the lover might have died of the Spanish flu, or been enlisted for a World War or something. Well, perhaps not, but the Italian postal service still hasn't got any quicker that's for sure… It's so frustrating not being able to get hold of her.

....

-Chiara, where've you been, I've been trying to contact you all afternoon!
-Francesca, what's wrong? Your voice is all quavery…
-Is it really? What do you mean?
-Oh come off it Franci, I know you too well. Don't play games with me. You're all excited about something. It's a guy isn't it? Who is he?
-Okay, let me compose myself. … Right, you know today I had the loss inspection for the last week's fire. Well, it went on all morning, and Conrad asked me to use my powers of persuasion and feminine charm with the assessor and take him out to lunch, to sound him out and find out a bit more about what he thought of the situation, that sort of thing!

-Well, so far nothing out of the ordinary, that's just about as far as men's understanding of female professional skills gets.

-No but that's not the point. He was nothing special to look at. Pretty average really: medium-height and build, short wiry hair, grey-silvery, peppery five 5 o'clock shadow look, in his early forties. He was wearing a dark grey, slim-fit Boss wool suit, two buttons - just a bit on the small side or him, with an open white shirt, no tie, and black brogues…

-Franci, for God's sake! You sound like Barbie dressing Ken. Did you take an X-ray too? Get on with the story!

-Well, okay, but I wanted to tell you what he looked like. It sets the scene.

-Did he have glasses?

-Police titanium frames, I'd say, and penetrating grey-blue eyes.

-These are all positives..What about the negatives?

-Well, I suppose he was a bit clumsy. He knocked a glass of mineral water over at the start of lunch – he was a bit nervy in my company; and he did slurp a couple of times when drinking his wine, and I couldn't help noticing he left some food on the side of his glass, but apart from that, well, he was just one of the nicest men I've ever met.

-Now, that's some confession from the Ice Queen of Sapporo! So what did you talk about?

-Well, it wasn't so much what he said; he was a listener, but he was always thoughtful in his replies and I found that really engaging, and he seemed to genuinely appreciate being in my company. He was completely different from other guys. And he's a voluntary ambulance driver for the 118 Emergency Service.

-Okay I get it, he's had his wake up call, something terrible in his life, personal tragedy maybe?

-Well, what do you mean by that? He did say he'd been a father and that was part of his growing pains.

-There you are then, Franci.

-Ah yes, you must be right. I was so swept off my feet by him, that comment didn't really register with me.

-Franci, you really do just live life in your own bubble, don't you? One day the bubble will burst. It always does.

-Okay, okay, Chiara, you're always right! Where are you anyway?

-Well, I'm at the gym. I couldn't answer the phone because I was having your personal training session with Daniele. You had an appointment with him at 4:30pm.

-Oh shit, that's the second lesson I've missed in a row.

-He said he was sure you wouldn't mind me filling your spot, so I jumped at the opportunity. And you're right, buns of steel. He's definitely my number one candidate for butt rape!

***

Fourteen

Burning Issues - The extraordinary story behind the scenes of the Gandalf Enchanted Garden Hotel

By our local correspondent Angelo Caduto

A dramatic fire broke out in the restaurant kitchen area of the Enchanted Garden Hotel on Thursday night, between two and three in the morning. This is just the latest event in a spate of fluke mishaps that have beset the hotel since its inauguration in May 2014.

Not least among these was the flooding of the bathroom in the deluxe themed balcony apartment, occupied at that time by Harry Potter celebrity, Daniel Radcliffe, VIP guest of honour for last season's opening. Mr Radcliffe allegedly slipped and broke his arm while entering the closet, missing the inauguration as a consequence. Other incidents have involved a near miss for a Russian guest who was almost hit by a falling roof tile as he stooped to pick up a mysterious-looking keyring in the hotel foyer. Rising damp and mould have caused allergic reactions to guests in some of the ground floor rooms, and in one case, a theming panel became totally detached from a bedroom wall, nearly crushing a couple during their amorous advances, and almost transforming their Saint Valentine's night of romance into tragedy. Some members of staff now believe the hotel to be jinxed, and are seemingly worried about returning to their jobs for the Easter bank holiday weekend. Others have suggested that, due to head office budget constraints, the Hotel had been short-cutting on basic maintenance, jeopardising its functioning and potentially placing guests at risk.

Yet the most extraordinary event so far, appears to be the fire in the hotel restaurant kitchen. While the cause of the blaze is still not clear - faulty cabling, an overheating fridge compressor, or a negligently switched on cooking hob – a subsequent explosion seems to have occurred at the exact moment a member of the security staff opened the emergency fire door from the outside. From video footage anonymously delivered to our press office, it would appear that the security office actually caused a second explosion by smoking a cigarette at the scene of the incident. The security officer in question, who is currently sedated and under observation in hospital, is reported to have permanent disfiguring to his head and face, but his life is not endangered.

The mystery cause of the fire is further compounded by allegations that the water sprinkler system failed to activate when the fire first broke out, which would have most probably prevented it from spreading at an early stage, and perhaps even the subsequent explosion from occurring. If this is found to be true, the Gandalf Group's reputation could be seriously damaged.

The Enchanted Garden Hotel belongs to the international hotel chain, Gandalf Hotels and Destination Resorts, specializing in holiday resort destinations for families. Last year, the group posted pre-tax profits of €155 million, as room revenues increased by 2.5%. It also entered into the top ten on Europe's Gold List for destination hotels, and this year it is competing for the accolade at global level. Thanks to the latest events and the Group's mission of offering extraordinary experiences to guests of all ages under company slogan "*Gandalf spells Magic*", the Enchanted Garden Hotel would appear to be adding an entirely new chapter to "weekend escapes and getaways"!

***

Fifteen

Three days, and still no news from Lemon Tart. I've spent the whole day mooning around at home. This was my day off. It could have been so different. I just chose to waste it. Tried to watch TV, tried to read the paper, tried to read a book, tried to catch up with my administrative work. The result: tried and failed; I'm too restless and weary. I had forgotten what it was to pine for something I can't have, to expose myself to my barest needs and my own fragility. Routine has been very convenient in all these years, that's for sure, and change stings like salt in an open wound. But I want it.

I wonder what all these red candles are around the apartment?

-"Traumschwarz!
- What, you're you calling me!? This is out of character. Have you forgotten it's your day off? Is this another toilet tantrum? The toilet paper is in the bathroom cabinet. I put a fresh eight-roll pack in there on Saturday morning!
-No, just put the recording on pause for a second. I need some information. And what's all this scented candle

business? You're not opening a recreational therapy center for depressed yogis in my living room!

-Well, no darling I'm not, you're quite right. You're a genius. Is that all you wanted? To insult my impeccable taste in interior design again?

-Well, we do have a minimal *Boffi* lounge suite and dining table, and we both agreed that the only exception to that would be the *Lalique Crystal Twin Vases* my mother gave us for our wedding present.

-The vases are *Venini* not *Lalique!* How many times do I have to tell you? You really should remember that, you might be jeopardising your inheritance. And FYI, the scented candles are *Versace Medusa*.

-Exactly, completely out of character.

-That's as may be, but we need them for Feng Shui.

-And who's he? You've not taken up Chinese, have you? And where have you hidden the dragons then, at your mother's?

-There you go again with your sarcastic piss-taking. I bet you haven't even noticed the pink triangle candles in the bathroom.

- What's all this in the bathroom? Yes, I'm doing time in here now. You've transformed it into a Gay and Lesbian Holocaust Memorial!

- I'm not even going to reply to that, but why is it that we always have our most significant arguments while you're bombing the porcelain? Anyway, they're there to get rid of excess fire energy in our lives. It's important to develop harmony and compassion through the correct balancing of energy in the home. According to Feng Shui, an overabundance of fire energy leads to disharmony and vexation. Wanda suggested I get them.

-Yes, and another thing it's bloody freezing in here. Why have you lowered the temperature in the daytime? You know I don't like the cold…. Wanda? That woman's completely bonkers. All her emancipation nonsense and crackpot ideas about men living in their lunchboxes. And she wears cherry red *Dr. Marten* boots at the age of seventy-two! And another thing… If you want to develop compassion, the first thing you do is suspend judgment, and the second thing is you listen!

-She's sixty-two, actually! She's a free spirit.

-Well, we operated on her daughter last week and she's forty-eight, so you can work that one out next time you're doing Giorgio's maths homework for him.

-Look, I'm not going to spend the whole day arguing with you. I've got enough on my plate as it is. Now that I'm listening , as you say, …..was there a reason for your call, or are you just complaining again because you're bored, and you need a sacrificial victim?

-Well no actually, I want to know where your desserts recipe book is, you know *The Wooden Spoon;* I'm going to cook a lemon meringue pie."

….

So much for her listening, she didn't even manage thirty seconds? She's hung up!

***

Sixteen

-"Benito, Franci calling. Have you seen that despicable article in the local rag? This is becoming my worst nightmare. It must have been that bitch, Anna.

-It's understandable to think that, and we all think the same thing, but there's very little we can do. She went to the trade union representative before she handed in her notice; she had accumulated seventy-eight days of vacation leave, which is over the permitted limit for her category, so as of today, she's on garden leave until the notice matures formally. She's also threatened to take us to court and sue us for mobbing and downgrading with her transfer to the hotel reception. So, basically she's stitched us up good and proper this time.

-Well, I can't accept this. We've got to find out which member of security passed her the video footage, and fire him.

-Listen, if there's a witchhunt to be conducted with public executions, I'll be the one doing the *auto-da-fè* in this company. That's my job. I've worked with security for more than twenty years. I know who the weak links are. It's just a question of time. But in any case, that is not going to redress the current situation; the cat's out of the bag and amongst the pigeons. It would be better if you focused on the loss assessment consultant and the cause of the fire with the Chief of the Fire Service, if you get where I'm coming from. Conrad is going to have to foot the bill for this one with the board. It was his idea to swear us to secrecy about the missing certifications. He'll just have to do his own dirty work for once.

-I guess you're right, but right now I'm totally furious. I need to take it out on somebody. I've always known she was a snake in the grass. I should have trusted my intuition and acted earlier.

-Okay Franci, but no collateral damage. If we play this one tight, we can stay afloat. Sometimes, it pays to be brutally honest. Your sins always find you out, remember!

-If it was any other day, you wouldn't have got away with that last line of yours, but…

-I've got it…It's just come to me in a flash. Here's the plan; bear me out: if I were in the firing line like Jeff, I would be making an amicable arrangement with the local newspaper, say, a small announcement printed in tomorrow's paper apologizing for the erroneous content of that slanderous report in today's article. That way, we avoid being put under the spotlight again. The Fire Chief won't have any problems signing off that a major electrical fault started the fire with the hob and short-circuited the sprinklers. Maybe you could find a way of dealing with the loss consultant, so that he agrees on that. And I'll come down on the security like a ton of bricks.

-So that's your version of honesty paying eh?..… corruption, bribery, mobbing and maybe a bit of skirt for good measure. I buy it. But seriously, I'll work on the damage loss assessor. He's a reasonable type of guy and I'm sure he'll see reason. Then of course, Jeff will have to appease the board. Are you going to speak with Jeff or shall I?

-I'll do it. I've known Jeff for a long time and he'll listen to me.

-Apart from our occasional run in, we really do see eye to eye on most things, don't you think Francesca? I've never really understood how that can be possible. Nothing as queer as folk, as they say!

-Indeed we do. Don't call the damage loss assessor till tomorrow. We don't want to appear too alarmed. Need to let the dust settle.

***

Seventeen

Thursday. Another night shift. After that awful day yesterday burning the lemon pie and fighting with Franci again, another dark night to reflect upon my miserable condition. And probably the best thing I've got to look forward will be the operating table...if I'm lucky, the adrenalin will help me pass the time. I wonder what tonight's splat movie will be? Another domestic violence stabbing, or a drunken driver having an extrasensorial perception crisis with a tree? That certainly keeps the voluntary ambulance drivers busy. In the medical profession, we spell compassion with a K that sits snugly in our bank accounts, but they give their time freely. You have to admire them. How do they do it? I'll be writing a sombre poem tonight.

(*Ting!*)

Oh, It's a message from my chatroom… Lemon Tart!

'Stormtrooper, sorry I missed you
Been away in Milan for a training course.
Just back
When are you free?'

Okay, I'm desperate but I'm not stupid. That message is adding insult to injury. Let's see who's calling the cards.

'On night shift at hospital
Free now'
'Come and meet me at the hospital
bar
Dessert in my luxury 5-star
penthouse hospital suite?'
'Great
I'll be there in half an hour.
Give me a number to call you'
'3426050741'
'I'll call in 5 minutes'
'Ok'

✼✼✼

Eighteen

-"No stop it, don't draw circles around my belly-button. It tickles"
-When I was a child, we used to say, "If a bus comes…", when you wanted someone to stop bothering you….
-What do you mean by that?
-So that the other person kept doing it until you said "Stop it!" But just give me one more kiss, and I'll recite a poem for you.
-Okay, please stop it…!

…..

"O lovely fragrant rose
Born on a summer's day,
Thou dost both damozels
And dames with envy sway,
Out of this furnace flame,
Sweet, rescue me, I pray;
From thoughts of thee Madonna, I ne'er cease,
And day and night I am bereft of peace!

-That's amazing *Stormtrooper*… please say it again, but this time whisper it into my ear. I want your sweet warm breath to ruffle the nape of my neck".

……

-"Who wrote it? Poetry is my passion, and this is a great one!

-It's the opening of *Rosa fresca aulentissima*, one of Italy's most famous 13th century medieval poems. The English had King Arthur and the Knights of the Round Table, but we had Federick II, the Duke of Swabia; he was Barbarossa's father.
-And?
-Well, Cielo d'Alcamo, who wrote it, was a court jester at Frederick's court. His nickname was *il Ciullo*, which falls somewhere between a shortened version of the name Marcelo and a vulgar reference to him being well-endowed, let's say. In this poem, an enamoured lover attempts to woo a virtuous maiden until she succumbs to his poetic charms and agrees to take his hand in marriage, but she certainly doesn't wait till marriage to lose her virginity.
-So he seduces her? How romantic! But you're not really called Marcello, are you?
-No, Edoardo.
-Thought so.
-And you're not Fiore, either.
-No, but I'm going to keep you guessing, Stormtrooper, Edoardo, *Marcello, il Ciullo*! Now, I know why the damsels and the dames couldn't resist him, just like me with you!!! So how do you know all this?
-Insomnia!
-Well, I've got a poem with roses too.. do you want to hear it?
-I'm all ears….

"They are not long, the weeping and the laughter,
Love and desire and hate:
I think they have no portion in us after
We pass the gate.

They are not long, the days of wine and roses:
Out of a misty dream
Our path emerges for a while, then closes
Within a dream".

-How true! Love, as life, is so fleeting indeed. I guess you've won this round of our epic battle! Who is it by?
-This is not a happy story. It was written by an Oxford student who was an alcoholic towards the end of the nineteenth century. His name was Ernest Dawson and he died very young. He gave the poem a Latin title, "*Vitae Summa Brevis Spem Nos Vetat Incohare Longam*" – The Shortness of life forbids us long hopes.
-Six hundred years of lovers' desperate yearnings bound in sweet-scented bouquets of roses. One craving to embark upon a life of love and passion, and the other rueing its transience. Little has changed, but whatever loves are won and lost, roses will always survive them. I have a strange sense of foreboding that is making me feel morose. I hope this won't be our destiny. I'm just starting to get an appetite for you, Lemon Tart!

. . . .

-Oh, there goes my hospital pager. That means I've got to go down to A&E immediately. It's 1:30 am. I don't know how long I'll be. But there must be an emergency and we'll probably need to operate.

-Well, listen I can make tracks, and we can catch up in the week.

-No, I'd like you to stay. You can't lock the door but no one will disturb you. There's only one other doctor on night call and she's in the room next door.

-Are you sure? I don't mind.

-No, please stay!

***

Nineteen

-"Now I'm all restless too, and I can't sleep. Certainly, if relationships were just based on passion, we'd have made more hay than the entire prairies of North America! It's past four in the morning, I wonder how long he'll be. What if my bard, Marcello, is not back before morning. He said he normally vacated the room before 7:30am. At least I know the way out. Lift by staircase B down to Floor -1, turn left, the second right into the changing rooms and showers, and from there I can exit directly into the parking area. I wish I'd brought a book to read.
(Ting!).
Ah, that's a message. It must be him.

"Just finished. Be with you in ten minutes."

……..
-"Oh?
-Oh?
-Sorry, I was…
-No, it's okay, really.
-I've got the wrong room. I should be next door. Sorry.
-Oh shit…."

…..

-"Ah, Edoardo…Thank God you're here. Listen, I think your colleague just came into this room by mistake. She opened the door, saw me, said sorry and made a quick exit.
-Yes, I know.
-What do you mean, you know?
-Well, I've just bumped into her in the corridor. She was smirking with her head lowered so I asked if everything as okay. And she said she'd seen you in my bed.
-And what did you say?
-The first thing that came into my head.
-Which was?
-Well, I just told her not to worry because you were a friend and you'd had some domestic issues and needed a place to sleep.
-No way, she won't believe that, it's far too obvious…what if she tells your colleagues?
-No, she won't do that. We're good friends. We've been working together for the last fifteen years. And she

knows that I know too much about her private liaisons too. She's having an affair with the director of oncology.

-Are you sure? I knew this would go pear-shaped. Put the table up against the door. I'll never sleep now.

-Well, it's too late to change things. Let me snuggle up to you again. In the morning, we can have breakfast together at my favourite bar…..

-Hmmm, that's nice!

❖❖❖

Twenty

-"Hello Mr. Ciullo?. Beato, it's Francesca speaking.

-Ah Franci, what a pleasant surprise, everything going well at your end? Listen, I'm not quite ready with the assessment yet, sorry I'm a bit late - I just have to make some final adjustments.

-Ah okay …well.. of course, I can imagine. Listen, the article that appeared in today's paper has aired totally unfounded and potentially damaging allegations against our company. It insinuated that the water sprinklers at our hotel had failed due to poor standards of maintenance. We're going to sue them.

-Well to be honest, I hadn't read the local paper report, but…

-Ah you hadn't?

-No, but as I was saying, from my point of view that's quite immaterial Francesca; your Fire Prevention

Certificates are in order and substantiated by the Fire Chief's report.
-Ah, they are?...I mean, yes, of course they are. Well, I was just ringing to make sure that these rumours would not affect our standing. This incident has been very stressful for us. And the timing of this article in the period leading up to the Easter Bank Holiday weekend could be a catastrophe.
-How's your security guard?
-Ah, well, yes, he's stable, thanks but we're very disappointed by his conduct, and there will be an internal inquiry…
-Look, as far as I'm concerned Francesca, there are no problems at all. I understand your concerns and you were right to raise them with me.
-Well, that's fine then. Thank you again Beato.
-Don't mention it.
-Are you in our area in the near future?
-Not for the moment, I'm afraid. I'm going to be back in head office for a while. We are restructuring by sector, and I'm responsible for developing a new fire assessment team for the hotels and catering industry. That means I'll be in Rome for some time.
-That's a shame. I was looking forward to catching up with you.
-Well, you never know. Take care Francesca, and I'll have the report sent by the end of today. Bye now
-Bye then.

***

Twenty-One

-"Fiore – what will you have?
-Just an empty croissant and a cappuccino. That will do me fine.
-With or without powdered chocolate?
-Relax Edoardo. I don't mind, whatever inspires you most.
-Okay, so that's two cappuccinos and two empty croissants, please!
-Come on Edo, we're not joined at the hip yet… You look like the type that would go for a Nutella cream croissant.
-You're right. One Nutella, and one empty croissant, thanks.
-Ah, look who's there? It's Edoardo Cassese *alias* Ed Case, the Policlinico's very own Poet Laureate.
-Morning Renato, what's all that about?
-Your poem is going to be posted on the Oncology Ward?
-Oh my God, you're not serious! This will be excruciating. Who told you that?
-Insider dealing! Let's see. How does it go?

"Newton befell that apple, and claimed his noble truth,
He bit it with such venom, and cracked his wisdom tooth!"

-Oh, go fuck and yourself Renato! There's no way it's going to appear on the Oncology Ward, believe me.

-See you on the wards tomorrow, then!
-You'll pay for this, and it'll cost you dearly. Mark my words.

…..

-What's all that about? Are you doctors at the hospital, or is this a remake of *Dead Poets* Society? You all seem a bit enlightened round here. What time is Robin Williams joining us for coffee?
-Oh come on Fiore, not you too! Listen, when I work nights, I hardly ever sleep. Sometimes, I write a few lines, short stories or poems, that sort of thing, just to pass the time. Well, a while back, I must have been having a really bad night because I saw an advert for a National Poetry Prize for health professionals, and I just sent my poem in for a joke.
-Well, the joke's on you now. So how did your colleague find out about it?
-No idea. He's got his finger in every pie, well almost!
-Yes, he was a bit of a slimeball. His eyes were all over me.
-Well, don't worry about him, he lost all his powers of discernment long ago. He's just got a one-track mind. That's why I didn't introduce you to him.
-Well your tact is much appreciated. I don't particularly want to meet him again.
-Anyway, back to the poetry. Last week I got a letter inviting me to attend a prize-giving and dinner, free

weekend in Ancona, down in the Marches. It's the third weekend in May.

-I love the Conero, that august white-stone cliff fringed with Mediterranean woodlands rising majestically above the ocean. I can smell the sea breeze just thinking about it.

-Well, how would it be if you joined me on the "strawberry tree promontory"?

***

Twenty-two

Today, I've been asked to give a presentation for our latest company Webinar Series dedicated to Women in Leadership. Its aim is to further understanding on how our company can tackle the gender gap in the effort to boost women leadership in the workplace. As the only Female Director in the Italian organisation, and the only Female Director of Health and Safety in the entire global operations at Gandalf, I feel particularly honoured to take the floor. But I've got to make an impact. I want my colleagues to really get to grips with just how chauvinistic and male-dominated our Italian society is. I'm going to start with an autobiography of my childhood using photographic evidence to capture my colleagues' attention and show how my early imprinting was formed through discipline and application. The only thing that worries me is that it's going to be a bit like preaching to the converted. So far, no male colleagues have even signed up for my presentation. I bet if I sent out a general email out saying that I would be appearing in my latest swimwear for the summer at the beach, I would suddenly be inundated by the company's testosterone-tormented troopers. Then, I thought it would be interesting to compare myself to the Greek Goddess, Artemis and her Roman succesor, Diana. Yes, I think it's so appropriate to make this allusion to Greek mythology and Roman deities, because that's where our culture originated. Not that women enjoyed political or many other freedoms in ancient times, and in modern times, the Greeks only gave women the right to vote in 1952. And wasn't it Aristotle who argued in the Hellenistic period that women were apt to bring disorder and evil, and were utterly useless? He is alleged to have said that he preferred to go to battle with the enemy rather than endure a woman's confusion around him. That part, I can really identify with, when I think of how the vast majority of my female colleagues conduct themselves at work. I mean, they just don't have analytical skills, and they certainly are more interested in what they are cooking for their husband's dinners than the company's ideals! Anyway, where was I? Oh yes, Artemis - she was the Greek goddess of the hunt, the wilderness, the moon and chastity; in Roman times she was represented by Diana, the patroness of the hunters and the countryside. No, come on, Franci, she was a triple deity with a capital "D" - she was Diana the Huntress, Diana the Moon, and Diana the Underworld. I think that this triple association represents me perfectly in my role with the Gandalf Group today: I'm the huntress when I'm battling with my male colleagues, fighting for greater equality through knowledge-based culture at work; then I'm Diana the Moon when I am a mother ruled by the natural life cycles of the universe. I see Diana the Moon essentially as representing female intuition and the warmth of a mother's instinct for protection, which I have often relied on as a team-builder and team leader; and finally, I'm Diana the Underworld; of course, here I'm the Goddess holding the key to knowledge, one who can distinguish between light and dark, offering right guidance and counsel, which is the very essence of our success in the highly-competitive corporate environment, and which undoubtedly distinguishes we women as leaders from our male colleagues. Moreover, I'm curious to see what impact the association of Greek and Roman Goddesses will have on my female colleagues globally, with the focus on envisualizing how we can use feminine grace to lever influence in a male-dominated environment.

Oh well, this is your life, Mrs Scarpa, so it's time to let the camera roll, and "ACTION"!

…...

-"…well, as I said, I came from a very average middle class family. I was the brainy kid with teachers for parents. A lot of pressure to get it right, from an early age. Here's a picture of me holding a rolling pin while I'm was cooking with my mother. I love that daisy-flowered apron I'm wearing. And here's another picture of me in my ballet costume playing the role of a Sugar Plum Fairy in the Ballet School Recital of the Nutcracker. I was just twelve at the time, and I'm particularly fond of this photo because it shows me with my golden locks of hair....of course, as I grew I moved away from playful frolicking to a solid science-based secondary education. I've always been fascinated by rules, logical analysis and procedures. I have found they keep people focused "on the straight and narrow path", and give them little opportunity for erring into the wilderness.....

.....so that brings me to the end of my presentation. Yes, my life has definitely been an experiential learning journey. I'd now like to give the floor to you to ask questions.

-How do you think your Diana analogy could be used to create leadership initiatives for both men and women?

-Thank you ...Is that Fridda from Stockholm? That's a perfect question. Of course, in our experience here in the north of Italy, women are not generally treated as equals, as I said, so the idea of showing Diana in her triple deity role serves to set up a paradigm for analysing patterns of behaviour and the role models we tend to take for granted in our day-to day operations in the workplace today....From there, it would be important to...."

...Well, it's been incredibly edifying to receive your feedback. Thank you all from the bottom of my heart for participating, and looking forward to seeing you next week."

....

Now that was a great morning. I think I really excelled and pulled it out of the bag. I always respond well to pressure. That's my performing days in ballet coming in useful again. It was a pity though that only six colleagues participated. We do have more than 150 hotels worldwide plus three regional office headquarters around the world. I'd have thought that such a critical challenge as women in leadership roles would have garnered a little more support than this. That just goes to show how ill-prepared we are for change and that prejudices run deep. I did appreciate Benito making an appearance; As HR manager, it was good for my morale. Fascist or not, he's a good listener. I must call Chiara to let her know how it went. She'll be proud of me.

…..Oh, she's not answering again. That is strange. Just lately, she's been playing hard to get! Let me text her again. God only knows when she'll be in touch.

"Chiara, where are you? Call me asap!"

Right, that's done, I'd better get down to some real work. Raffaele has been pestering me all week about drawing up a new manual for kitchen cleaning procedures. He wants a two-tier procedure, categorically separating the cleaning phase from the sanitisation phase. He said we were lagging way behind with international standards on the sanitisation phase. Of course, I would add a signing-off stage after the completion of each cleaning phase for all the cooking equipment. It will take longer, I know, but we can't take any risks after last week. We don't want the

National Geographic including us in their latest article on volcano hotspots, do we? Anyway, I've always thought it curious that men should be interested in developing procedures for cleaning kitchens…

Ah, there's Chiara now.

"-Chiara, thank God for that. I've just done an amazing presentation about tackling inequality and developing women leadership in our company. It was a webinar and my colleagues participated from all over the world.

-What you're saying is that they switched on their webcams?

-Yes, well I'm so excited about it. It means I'm really part of the cutting edge drive for change in our company. You know, I really do think I'll be ready for an international position within a couple of years. All my female colleagues respect me and expect so much of me. They look up to me Chiara. I think it's because they know that I don't care a damn about playing the cool corporate cat…And I have you to thank for that. You're an infinite source of inspiration for me. So what've you been up to this time? I tried to call again and you didn't answer.

-I was at A&E.

-What? Why didn't you say? Nothing serious, I hope?

-Thomas.

-Oh, I see, our boys are such a worry nowadays. What happened?

-He's got a chipped tooth and broken nose?

-No Chiara, that's awful. What on earth happened?

-He was bullied by a group of kids. They kicked him in the head!
-Well how many of them were there?
-Five.
-And they stole his phone.
-No, not his Apple iPhone 11, the 128 Giga one? It was nearly new for Christ's sake.
-Is he going to be okay?
-He's shocked, bruised and feeling sorry for himself.
-I can imagine. Listen, were they Italian? I've read some terrible things about violent Eastern European teenage gangs in the local press. Did you have a tracking app on the phone? That way the police will catch them.
-Tom said they were all Italian, fifteen or sixteen year olds, and they picked on him because of his green hair.
-The little bastards. If ever something like this happens to Giorgio, I'll kill them, I swear I will.
-Tom said they were on drugs and that was why they were after his phone.
-Scum is scum. It doesn't matter if they are Italian or foreigners. Well, I hope they get them soon. So where are you now?
-On our way home?
-Okay. Listen, I'll call you later to see how you are, then I can tell you more about my presentation. Give Tom a kiss from me. He's a tough kid, don't let this get him down.
-Yeh!
-At least you've got Paolo to set his teeth straight!
-Bye Franci.

***

Twenty-Three

-"Stormtrooper, is that really you calling me on the phone again. It's so out of character.
-Yes, you're right, and as it's almost a week since I last saw you, I thought it's about time we had a catch up fight on the telephone.
-Ah, it doesn't feel that long. I suppose it must be because your smell lingers with your socks and undies on the bathroom floor. Listen, they are meant to go in the washing basket, not in the vicinity. In my next life, I'm definitely going to marry a basketball player. Everything okay with Edo, I hope? Remember you said you'd pick him up from football practice this afternoon. I've got yoga-bike and I really don't want to miss it. It's almost a month since I last went. And remember to put the dinner in the oven. Your mum has sent us a lasagne over, and so you …
-Franci, cool it. I've got everything under control. I'll be waiting outside the football club at 6.15pm, in good time, don't worry. I know how he hates the fact that you're always late, so I'm going to pride myself on being early.
-Here we go, Mr. Perfect…
-Hey, listen, I've got something incredibly funny to tell you.

-Really? Go on then?

-It's about my "smart aleck" friend and colleague, Renato.

-What then?

-Well yesterday his son, Massimiliano, got himself into deep trouble. Law and order.

-What does that mean?

-Another of my colleagues, whose daughter Sasha is the same age, said the police caught him red-handed with a stash of hashish and €550 in his pocket, arrested him and took him to the juvenile prison. It seems that he not only has a drug problem but that he's also a bit of a teenage pusher. He's only sixteen. You know that since he was thrown off the football team for kicking a boy in the back while he was on the floor last year, his life has taken a turn for the worse. He's been going to a psychoanalyst for two years because of his aggressive tendencies, but he's obviously still completely out of control. They released him later thanks to Renato's contacts. He's good friends with the Chief Judge at the Juvenile Court, but in any case, he'll be appearing before the examining magistrate on Monday to decide what measures to take next… Well, haven't you got anything to say about that? It's incredible.

-No, I'm speechless.

-What? You?

-He must have been one of the kids that smacked up Tom yesterday. Chiara's got to know this.

-What's that, Tom got beaten up?

-Yep, broken nose and smashed tooth. And they stole his iPhone.
-Small world isn't it? So, why do you think Little Mad Max got into this mess?
-I've got no idea, but I blame the parents. Remember to put the lasagne on for 25 minutes at 180°. I'll be back around 8.30pm.

***

Twenty four

-"Hey, papa, thanks for picking me up. And you're on time.
-Yes, I was on mornings today, so it's no problem. How did your training go?
-It was okay, I suppose.
-Well you don't sound too happy. Did something happen?
-No, it's not football, that's okay.
-What is it then?
-Well you know that girl Elisa at school?
-The one you like and have ice cream with?
-Yeh, well we've had a fight, and she said she didn't want to see me anymore.
-Oh that's bad. Why did she say that?
-Well, she said all I talked about was football and playing Fortnite with my friends.
-And?

-And she's not into football or Playstations. She's into pop songs by Nali?

-Who?

- Nali, you know Annalisa, she's a pop singer, and I'm into rap, like Mr Rain.

-Okay, that's all sounds very interesting, but you can have different tastes you know.

-She's into sweet-scented perfumes too. They're really sickly and they make me feel nauseous. And she said I had bad breath!

-Did you brush your teeth? You know that your mum is always reminding you about that?

-Yes, but it was just after Tom had given me a bit of his cheeseburger, and she said she didn't want to kiss me.

-Well, Giorgio, girls are pretty sensitive. Make sure you've got some chewing gum or mints with you next time.

-Dad, I don't want to speak to her anymore.

-Hey come on. Sulking won't make things better. If you like Elisa then you have to play their game. With girls, you need to learn to be patient, accept all their criticisms, and be nice to them whatever. It's the only way I know how to get what I want from your mother, but in the end, it works.

-Well, I told her I didn't like her stinky perfumes.

-Well do you still like her?

-Yeh, but.

-Okay, let's do this.. You're going to have to let this one settle for a while, but on our way home tonight, we are going to buy her a nice fragrance at Accessorize, okay? And when she starts to throw you long furtive glances, you go up to her really proudly and give her this new scent and say you're sorry. How about that?

-Well I'm not going to speak to her all next week.

-Just do it when you feel you're ready. There's no rush. ..Jump in then.

…

-So how's Tom?

-He left early. His dad came to pick him up and they went straight to hospital.

-Tom's going back to hospital? But surely he wasn't at football practice with a broken nose, was he?

-What papa? Tom hasn't got a broken nose. He's great and he scored three goals in training. His dad picked him up early because they've gone to San Raffaele hospital in Milan. His mum had to have an operation today.

***

Part Three

The Day of Reckoning

***

One

-"Giorgio, are you going to tell mama or shall I?
-Papa, I think it's better if you do it.
-What are the two of you rabbiting on about?
-Franci, Chiara is in hospital at San Raffaele in Milan. She had an emergency operation today. She went for a scan yesterday, and they kept her in overnight.
-But she …What? Giorgio can you go and play with your Playstation please, I need to talk in private with your papa.
-Yes mama…but what papa wants to say is that she had an operation today to remove a cancer. Tom told me everything. And Tom hasn't got a broken nose either.
-Oh my God, Edo, are you serious?
-Yes, dead serious.
-Where? I mean where did they operate.
-Frontal lobe, left hemisphere, just behind her left eye.
-Is it that serious?
-It's that serious. I've spoken to Paolo about it. She's already conscious and she'd like to see you tomorrow.
-Yes, of course….but I just don't understand. Well what type of cancer is it?

-They don't know yet, they've got to get the histological on that.
-So what do you think it is?
-Let's wait and see.
-But you know, don't you?
-Ok, it's almost certainly a glioblastoma. That's a grade IV malignant cancer.
-Do people survive that?
-No, if they're lucky they get a brief period of remission after removing the tumour.. She most probably won't be here in 18 months.

……

-Stormtrooper, can we sleep in the same bed tonight?
-Come on then Franci, it's been a long day.
-And what did Giorgio say about Tom?
-At least that one has a happy ending. He's fine. Chiara made up the whole story because she didn't want you to worry about her.

***

Two

There are times in your life when the gabbling monkey in your head falls silent. This is one of them. It's Saturday morning and I'm driving along the *Serenissima* motorway towards Milan with Edo. My mind is focused and calm. I know exactly what will happen to Chiara. She's going to recover from her operation, go through hell with radiotherapy and chemo, and she'll be able to attend any unfinished work family and children before her tumour grows back. Her greatest pain will be wrenching herself from the invisible umbilical cord embracing her children's blissful play in the Garden of Eden. This type of cancer is unaware of the word remission. She will hold no fear of dying, and make her graceful exit on the wings of her guardian angels.

-"Here we are. Now Giorgio, can you and Tom go and play in the common area by the reception, while I speak with Chiara for a few minutes?
-Yes mama.
-Chiara, my beautiful Chiara. What have they done to you?
-Typical, I knew you'd be here first… It's a big patch over my eye, I know. I look like "Polyphemus meets Galatea - the Sequel", but that doesn't mean you have to stare at me like a Gorgon.
-Can I give you a hug?
-Well, I'm a bit fragile, and I'm bloated because of all the cortisone shots, but go on, just a gentle one.
-That's better.
-The consultant surgeon said the operation was a 100% success, and they were able to totally remove the tumour. So, I'm one of the lucky ones. By the way, that's the last time we say that word. From now on it's "the gift", okay.
-Sure, let's make it positive.

-To get to "the gift", they actually had to drill a little window in my skull and remove the bone, and then they closed the porthole again. They said it would heal over. I can't wait to see that. So don't be surprised if I change my name to Lily Frankenstein. And they only shaved one side of my head. It reminds me of the days when I was a "Goth" at uni! Only wearing black…what an omen. Am I boring you Franci?
-No Chiara, I'm just listening to your story.
-Well, your eyes are welling up with tears. It's okay to cry. I don't want you to put on a brave face for me. And the last thing I want is for people to feel sorry for me. Feeling sorry is the projection of your own unresolved misery onto another person. So if you want to cry, you can, but go and stand by the window, put on my headphones and listen to Queen singing "Don't Stop me Now". I've got it all ready for you, thanks to Andrea my nurse. He's wonderful. He's only 24, and I swear I've never met such a warm, giving and kind person in my life.
-No Chiara, it's okay, it's just a moment. It'll pass.
-It's hard isn't it? I know. I'm sorry too. But this is where I'm up to. Don't you want to know what happened?
-Well, you don't have tell me, it's okay, really.
-No I'd rather tell you than have you hear it from someone else.
-I was watching TV on Wednesday evening after dinner with Paolo. There wasn't much on, so Paolo said let's have a beer and watch Game of Thrones on Netflix. We're up to Season Six. So, I said "I'd love a beer", only I said "fear". I literally couldn't say the word beer, the

"fear" word just kept coming out. I didn't have a headache or anything. Paolo wanted me to go down to A&E immediately, and I said, no I'll sleep on it and see how I am in the morning. I was really looking forward to my Corona Extra and fresh lemon, and I was sure it would just pass. On Thursday morning when I woke, I had completely lost all movement of my lips and I couldn't even keep my breakfast in my mouth, and I had a fixed expression around my eyes. I was having a sort of progressive paralysis.

-Well your okay now, aren't you? I mean I haven't noticed any speech impediment?

-Of course I'm okay now, Franci! If you're Dr Watson, can you tell the nurse I want Sherlock back immediately. I can get a bit slow and slurry with my speech when I'm tired but that's all solved. Anyway, this time Paolo insisted on me going to A&E at San Raffaele Hospital. He was really worried and he didn't want me spending a day in the waiting room at our local hospital. This is a center of excellence he said, and they gave me a brain scan immediately. So here we are. They operated on Friday morning, in less than 24 hours. That must be a record for a state hospital.

-So what caused the speech impediment?

-Franci, you don't have to be a genius to work that out.

-Well, I know it was the "tum…", I mean the "gift", but..

-Well, I think the doctor called it apraxia or something. And he said I might get aphasia or dysarthria whatever that means; all these "a-something" words, but all I want right now is "a coffee". All they let me have here is that milky whitewash they call tea. It's never hot when they bring it and the sterilised milk is enough to even be a turn off for a tealeaf.

-Chiara, don't please, you're cracking me up.

-And I shouldn't laugh either because it makes my head hurt.

-Oh, here's Paolo.

-Listen Chiara, can I get you anything? I need the bathroom.

-No, we're fine. Franci, we were wondering if you'd mind having Tom and Matilde for the weekend, so that I can stay here with Chiara. If it's okay, I'll pick them up on Sunday afternoon. We don't want my parents getting involved at this stage. They're too old for that, and Chiara's father is too far away, and it's not practical.

-Listen, it's no problem. They can stay as long as you like. If you give me your keys then I'll go to your home and get some clothes for them. When do you think you're coming home?

-Franci, bring me a coffee from the bar, will you? The doctors said I'll be out on Tuesday.

-No, darling, they said Tuesday or Wednesday, all being well.

-As early as that?

-I'm under observation now; the surgery went well. If my tests come back okay and there are no complications, there's no reason for me stay here. I'd rather convalesce at home.

-Okay then, I'll be back in a few minutes.

***

Three

-"Matilde, tomorrow we're going to bake a cake together, would you like that? Tom, how about going to McDonalds tonight? You and Giorgio can get a cheeseburger?
-Mum, really? That's so cool!
….
-Aunty Franci, when will mummy die? I know she's going to die. I can feel it.
-Shut up Matilde, she's not your aunty, anyway. She's mum's best friend, that's all. And mum's not going to die.
-That's not true, you're just lying.
-No, I'm not.
-You don't know anyway. You're just stupid. I hate brothers.
-Hey guys, come on, it's been a long day, another five minutes and we'll be home. Why don't you tell me what you want from McDonald's, then I'll ring Edo, and he'll order it for us? When we get home, dinner will be waiting for us. How about that?
-Mum can Tom and I play Fortnite after dinner?
-Of course you can, but not for too long. You know it's lights out at 10.30.
-Well Tom, I must say that I'm so happy that you didn't really get bullied and no one stole your iPhone. Your

mum is such a character when she wants to keep a secret. She had me fooled, that's for sure.
-Francesca, you know I didn't get beaten up last week, but it did happen actually.
-What do you mean? When?
-Well, last summer when you were on holiday, it was just after my twelfth birthday, and a group of kids from another school cornered me in the park when I was skateboarding. They burst my lip and gave me a black eye, and started kicking me when I was on the ground. Then a man came and stopped them. So they didn't get my phone, but I had to have three stitches.
-Your mum never told me that.
-That's cos' she was out shopping when it happened and she felt bad about it. Dad had a big fight with her and called her a selfish cow.
-And where was your dad?
-He was out riding his bike with his friends.
……

-Giorgio, now that's Tom's here for the weekend, what do you want to do on Sunday? Remember, it's Elisa's birthday and Giuseppina rang me to invite you to her party. Perhaps, you can both go.
-No mum.
-What? No? Simple as that?
-No!
-What does that mean?
-It means me and Tom are going to go skateboarding in the park.

-Oh, everything okay?.....
-Francesca, Giorgio doesn't speak to her anymore.
-Are you sure? I'm going to have to speak to Giuseppina about this. Elisa will be terribly upset. What am I going to say?
-It was Elisa who decided.
-Tom, no it wasn't.
-Yes it was, she said you had cheesy breath. Ha!
-Well I don't care anyway.
-Hey that's enough, we're home now.

***

Four

-"Francesca, good morning, Jeff calling.
-Oh morning Mr Conrad, I mean Jeff, everything okay?
-I just wanted to thank you for doing such a great job with the incident. The board gave me a hard time, but things should be okay, there. Are you okay?
-Jeff, I just needed a day off to recharge my batteries. There's been a lot going on in the past weeks. Now that we're out of crisis management. I'll be back on Wednesday. Any news on Stewart?
-No news is good news, so he should be back with us after the annual conference. Did you say Wednesday? Could it be Tuesday afternoon? I'd really appreciate you being for our team meeting, especially now that we're scheduling repairs for the final assault before the Easter

re-opening. Without Stewart, you're the only person who can handle it.
-I know, I'll see what I can do.
-Thanks Francesca. Everything okay? You do sound a bit flat.
-Yes, all is fine.
-Bye then. See you tomorrow.
-Bye.

***

Five

-"Lemontart, Can you speak? It's StormyEd!
-That's a cute nick… like it. Yeh, I'm free. Good to speak on the phone. In future, better if you text first though.
-Okay, you're right. I got a bit carried away with myself there. I haven't seen you for ten days.
-I'm still recovering from the last time…
-Listen, I'm free tonight because it's the Annual Junior Anaesthetists Leaving Party, which I always go to. I thought we could have dinner together and then put in an appearance … it's in a country villa just outside Vicenza.
-So why did you only call me now, if you knew about it before?
-My colleague has cancelled, because he thinks he's coming down with the flu'. I've only just found out I'm free.
-So is this Episode III: Revenge of the Sith?
-Have you been studying the Saga?

-Sure have!
-So tonight my mission will be to rescue you from General Grievous…
-Your colleague, Renato!
-Could be, there's a real story there.
-What do you mean?
-Well, he's had some of his own medicine, lately…
-Really?
-Yeh, his son has been arrested and charged with drug pushing - hashish.
-Hey, that's a force to be reckoned with…
-Your streets ahead of me at this game, Lemon Tart. Are you free then?
-I've got a birthday party celebration but I can feel a temperature coming on too, and I might have to cancel! So what's the plan?
-Can we meet outside the station 7:30pm? Then we head towards Vicenza; I'll find a place for dinner on my app. After, we'll have time to show up at the party for an hour or so. And then…?
-That's the interesting part!
-How does that sound?
-If it's going to be a memorable "And then…?", I'm up for it.
-My battleship or yours?
-Let's use mine; I've got my new Subaru Ascent station wagon. Company car. It's got great boot space. Might come in handy.

-Ready for take off. I'll see you at the station. You shouldn't have any problems seeing me. My lightsaber will be on full beam.
-I'll be looking out for it, have no fears. But it's your hilt I'm worried about, not your beam!"

....

-"So Ed, tell me, who were those two students of yours, you know the two sisters that are both infatuated with you...
-Ah, yes Bea and Isabella, we call them Beauty and the Beast – because of their characters - not their looks of course, they're identical twins. They've always done everything together, right from day one. Inseparable.
-Well I was thinking you could set up a little separatist movement of Clonetroopers with them...
-Come off it Fiore, they're nice girls, but they really are totally naïve when it comes to men.
-Well, my temperature is running a bit high again, so perhaps we should pull over into the lay-by. Are you ready to engage in battle?
-No, not on the motorway, that's way too risky.
-Stormtrooper, you're very conservative aren't you? You were all up for it when you were calling the cards in the hospital...but now!
-Imagine if we got caught. I can just see the headlines in the local paper.
-"Doctor caught with his pants down on public highway, claimed he was performing mouth-to-mouth

resuscitation". ..No, eh? Perhaps not… Okay, what if we head for the castle when we exit the motorway? I know a secluded area, where nobody will disturb us.
-Haven't I heard those words before somewhere?
-Well yes, you did say something quite similar at the hospital a couple of weeks back.
-Anyway, at least it's a better idea than your original plan.
-I'm just not sure how much longer I'll be able to hold out."

….

-"I love it when the windows steam up, don't you?

….

-Ed, listen, there's someone out there. Look, a light - it's someone with a torch. Quick get your trousers on.
-Christ, not the carabinieri!
-There's a fucking enormous dog too…It looks like a Rottweiler.
-Hey! You in there! I don't care what you're up to, that's none of my business.
-Edo, don't open the window.
-But you're not doing it here. I've taken down your number plate, and if I ever see you in these parts again, I'll be calling the police and charging you for trespassing. Now, fuck off!
-Thank God for that… sorry, mate, we just pulled over for a beer together.

-Well fuck off and have your beer somewhere else. You dirty bastards. Your lot make me sick with all with all your fornication and paper handkerchiefs. Last week, I had to take Tarzan to the vets; he nearly choked to death on one of your fucking condoms.
-Two minutes, and we'll be out of here.
-You can go and fuck yourselves all the way to Australia for all I care."

…..

-"Shite, that was hi-la-ri-ous Edo!
-That's one way of putting it Fiore, you're right about that. Next time though, perhaps we can book a room in a hotel.
-Or an afternoon at a B&B; I know a good place. It's called Margy's Home. They charge a minimum of two nights but they're very discreet. The owner thinks of herself as a bit of a *maitresse*, hoarding all the illicit sex and sleaze secrets of our entire libertine province.
-And you're a bit of an expert too!
-What's that supposed to mean? You're hardly in a position to call the virtue card, are you?
-Sorry Fiore, you're right. This just shook me a bit. Are you still on for Ancona?
-You bet, it's only a couple of weeks away. And I'm writing you a rose story for it.

***

Six

-"Oh Aunt Dot, is that you again? Lovely to hear from you.

-Yes, it's me. I've changed the batteries for my hearing aid and it's made such a difference. I can hear you perfectly today.

-Well that is good. So how have you been keeping?

-Well, it's been such a lovely Spring, lately. It hasn't rained for a week now and the temperature has been up in the seventies. That's so unusual for this time of year. And you know what? My laburnum is spectacular with all its golden tassels waving in the wind. It looks so carefree and irreverent – and then there's the hawthorn too. Yes, this year they're both exceptional. And I've been back on my bird count. This week, I've been able to record redwing and fieldfare sightings – yes, they're back, which is reassuring. And the tits are in abundance: blue tits and great tits. Of course, the common garden thrush has been decimated; we hardly see them these days. That's saddening. How about you? Seen any more black caps?

-No Dot, but I can hear them warbling away in the trees, that's for sure.

-Ah yes, and I think there's a couple of menacing magpies down at the bottom of the garden. They seem to be nesting in the hazel tree.

-Well, you don't sound too happy about that.

-No, I'm not, because they raid the small birds' nests and steal their eggs and chicks. And you know what, the fat block feeder lasts twice as long now as it did in the winter. The blue tits must be feeding on the insects and grubs now. But sadly, I haven't seen any chaffinches this year. They used to be one of the most popular garden birds up to twenty years ago. Then they started to decline. It must be the insecticides. It is awful. And the butterflies are back, more than usual, I think.

-Well, I hope they're being careful, otherwise some of your song birds will be making a feast out of them. Has your gardener been back?

-Well, he's been to the dentist and he didn't come yesterday so he must still have toothache. He had a bad tooth all last week. That's Edward, he's my next door neighbour's gardener. I prefer him to Geoff, because he does the lawn-mowing and he gives me fresh eggs. But he doesn't always take out the long grass among the shrubs. He's a bit slow.

-Sorry Dot, is that Edward your next door's gardener or Geoff, your regular gardener? I'm getting a bit confused here.

-No Edward. Geoff never even sees the long grass. But the problem with Edward is that he only does what he wants to. When I say to him to do the long grass first, and he leaves it till last, or he doesn't even bother to do it. All gardeners are the same. They just do what they want to. Take it or leave it.

-Well how's your leg been? Have you been getting in plenty of walking now the weather's warmer?

-Well the pain's no better, you know. But I'll just have to grin and bear that. When you were born I nearly missed

the news. I was sponging down the carpet on the stairs and the phone rang. And I said to myself, "I bet that's the headmistress, Miss Dillsworth again, I'm not going to answer it". She's got such a habit of ringing at the most inconvenient times. But then I thought I ought to, and I was just about to say something awful, when your dad told me the big news.
-That's a fond memory.
-It is!
-And is Roland still doing your shopping runs?
-Of course he is. But Peter gave me a some lettuce last week and it was very poor quality. I had to throw half of it away. So I'm going to have to ask him to get me one of those big lettuces, because they last much better. But then I'll probably have to throw half of that away too because it's too much for me.
-Sorry is that Roland or Peter?
-No Roland. Peter's my next door neighbour on the other side.
-So you've got Beele and Peter as neighbours? And where does Roland live?
-Roland's across the road, two doors up.
-It's all getting a bit confusing with Peter, Beele, Geoff, Edward and Roland. You seem to be spoilt for choice for male suitors.
-Well, I hardly think so, but I am lucky; they're always popping round to see how I am.
-And have you sorted out your emails?
-Well no, that's too much for me. I'm definitely not your digital aunt.

-You have to find a way of emptying your mail box otherwise you can't receive any more mails.

-Well I don't know, I cancel them all as they come in, so I don't know what it can be. Someone told me to try unplugging everything for a day, so I did that. And now it's asking me to login again with my name and password. Well, I don't know what my login name and password are.

-You must have written it somewhere on a chit of paper. Have you tried looking in your writing cabinet?

-No, but I will. It just got me too depressed yesterday, but I'm determined to do it. And how've you been? Your dad said you're separating from your Italian wife. I'm very sad about that you know. Are you sure it's for the best?

-Well, it wasn't my choice, Aunt Dot, so there's not much I can do I'm afraid. It's a bit of hard time for me too. I was thinking about coming back to the UK, actually.

-Oh no, you mustn't. You can't do that. What about your children? Promise me that you'll stay over there. You haven't lost your job have you?

-No, that's okay at least, but I've taken some time off to think things through. I'd got myself into a right state.

-Well, your dad had a problem with alcohol, when he was younger too. Now, don't you worry, it'll be alright, if you have the courage to face your problems. Don't blame yourself, otherwise it will become your excuse for wallowing in self-pity, and that never made the world a better place. If you want my advice, right now the most important thing in your life is your children. If you move away, you'll won't see them grow up and you'll spend

your life regretting it. It took me a lifetime to accept that I was different from most women of my time, and now the guilt and torment that haunted me for so many years after Madeleine died will soon be buried along with my bones. And you must accept being who you are too.
-Thanks for your advice, Dot. You're very wise.
- Live your life for who you are today, my dear Stewart, because there will come a time when you can only sit and watch at the window as others live theirs. And when that time comes, you spend most of your time fighting not to you fall into the cauldron of your own confabulations. Remember, the hardest judge of your character is always the person inside your own head. Anyone who says any different is lying."

***

Seven

Tonight I'm going to learn the technique of Transcendental Meditation. It's a really deep and powerful meditational practice. I thought I could learn it and then teach Chiara. It's going to be important for her to have a way of dealing with her suffering and staying focused on what she's still got to live for. It's quite different from doing Kundalini Yoga Kriyas. It doesn't involve any focus on breathing or chanting or excruciating asanas. It's based on a simple technique, which takes you beyond your thinking state of mind to release you into a deep state of inner peace. It uses a silent mantra that you repeat inside your head and you only need to practice it for twenty minutes at a time, recommended twice a day. You can even do it sitting on a chair. Never mind kundalini-bike. I'm definitely not going to tell Wanda about this, she'll be raging!

Ah, here we are. I'm in a sort of waiting room. It's a bit dank and smelly, doesn't look like anyone's been here for a while. The room needs airing. Ah, and that must be a picture of the yogi, Mahesh Maharishi, who founded the TM technique.

-"Okay Mr Cagliero, goodbye. Thanks for coming. It was a real pleasure meeting you and I'm so glad you've chosen our programme for your company. You won't regret it. We've done a huge amount of empirical research worldwide proving that our Creative Science Technique really does work. I'm looking forward to starting our programme next week.
-Goodbye then, Gustavo.
-See you Monday".

...

-"Ah, so you must be the delightful Mrs Scarpa. I'm Mr Losso, but please call me Gustavo.
-So, that Cagliero is an entrepreneur. I'm impressed; he's just signed up for a course for three hundred employees starting next week. We work a lot with companies, and

have achieved extraordinary results with improved rates of concentration and higher level of productivity. The difference between our technique and other meditational techniques is that we practice a science. And we have evidence to prove that it works. That's why it's popular with corporations today. So what do you do Mrs Scarpa?

-Well actually, I'm Health and Safety Director at Gandalf Hotels and Destination Resorts Group. Our regional offices are based at the Enchanted Garden Hotel just outside the city.

-Ah yes, I know it well. Read about you in the paper a couple of weeks back, a fire or something.

-Indeed, it's all resolved now, and fortunately we'll be open for the Easter bank holiday weekend.

-That is good. So what do you know about Transcendental Meditation?

-Well quite a bit actually. I've been moving in holistic energy circles for a few years now.

-We are growing very fast and many famous entrepreneurs and TV personalities swear by it. It's just huge in the States: the David Lynch Foundation, Arianna Huffington, Cynthia McFadden, and the list just keeps on growing. What makes it so special is the fact that it's so easy to do, in a couple of lessons you can master the technique. We don't even attempt to build any critical knowledge of your mind, or develop any particular self-awareness skills. Basically, it's the number one way to take stress out of your life forever, reducing blood pressure, hypertension and preventing cardio-vascular disease. And we've done widespread scientific testing under controlled conditions to prove it. I've got hundreds of pages here if you want to read up on it. Be my guest. So Mrs Scarpa…

-Francesca, call me Francesca, please.

-So Francesca how did you hear about us?

-Actually from a colleague at work. Rebecca - she's your niece.

-Oh… and how is she? I've haven't seen her for a few years. I've been very busy. That's good. Please give her my regards.

-I will, certainly.

-And is it for yourself or your company that you're interested in a course in TM?

-Well neither really. You see my best friend has a cancer, and I want to teach her the technique. She's not fit to come here at the moment, but I know she really would benefit from it.

-Well, listen that's perfect. Maybe I can give you a special discount for her then.

-That's very considerate of you.

-So, ,do you know how it works then?

-Well, you teach me how to meditate with a personal mantra, I believe.

-That's absolutely right. You've have done your homework well. But first, I always recite a Hindu prayer. We're not a religious order or anything like that. We're not interested in that. We are result-driven and just want the good news to spread by word of mouth. But we recite the prayer as a token of our respect to Yogi Maharishi, and it helps put us in the transcendental mindset.

-He's the founder of TM, right?
-Precisely. So have you decided? Would you like to receive your own personalised mantra?
-Yes of course, you don't need to convince me any further. Your preaching to the converted here - I'm all for this, one hundred percent.
-Okay,; I'm going to recite our prayer. I want you to hold these rosary beads. Just relax. You don't have to try to do anything. When I ask you to repeat your mantra, I want you to close your eyes and recite it under your breath three times. It's your own personal mantra and you mustn't tell it to anyone else. It's on this piece of paper. Ready?
-Ready!

....

-As Maharishi said: "And no prayer will go in vain. You have to knock and the door will be opened", and now I want you to enter into the plain of unity consciousness and unified wholeness; for this is God's realisation, the supreme realisation, so now please say your mantra three times, Francesca:
-"Kyrin…. Kyrin…. Kyrin.."
-Thank you, do you feel okay?
-Yes.
-Right, now just sit peacefully and repeat those words in your mind for a few minutes, for as long as you feel comfortable, and when you're done just let me know.

……

-Right, I'm returning…
-Okay, now I just want you to calmly come back to the real world, gently does it…
-Well, Gustavo, that was amazing! At one point I saw seagulls flying over the sea.

……

-Francesca, it's not important what you see or think. You just let these thoughts pass. Don't try to observe them in any way. So, good, well done, you did it for about fifteen minutes, which is pretty impressive for a first time. Okay, now I just want you to calmly come back to the real world, gently does it…
-Okay I'm back. You know, I almost fell asleep for a minute or two.
-Of course, that can happen; it just means you really relaxed. You obviously needed that. You know theta waves, which you need for deep meditation, are very close to the brain's delta wave, which you experience in deep dreamless sleep. Well you didn't snore anyway.
-I should nope not, I never have done.
….

-Good, now before you go, we just have to settle the financial aspect of your membership.
-Of course.

Okay, so that's nine sixty, and that includes coming back in a week's time for the second part of the meditation lesson. At the same time, okay for you?

Okay sure. So, it's nine sixty for the membership - the subscription fee, right? And what about the cost of the course?

-No, Francesca, it's just nine sixty, altogether.

-Well, here it is then, I've got a twenty euro note here. Have you got the change?

-Francesca, sorry there's been a misunderstanding. Nine sixty is nine hundred and sixty euros.

-Ah..well, I'm sorry..I feel so stupid… I completely misunderstood…right.

-Well, that's no problem..don't worry. You can complete the payment next week. But what can you give me now? Normally people pay at least a fifty percent deposit the first time.

-That's a bit messy for me actually. I've only got twenty euros on me right now. Look, can we do this another time, even tomorrow? I'll go to the bank and make an ATP withdrawal and we can arrange to meet somewhere. I can come here if you like, tomorrow at 7.00pm. How does that sound?

-If you like, I can accompany you to the ATP.

-Listen, Gustavo, I'm sorry, I just haven't got time right now. I'm late for dinner as it is and I've got to cook for my twelve year old boy and my husband.

-Oh, I see. Well that's fine then Francesca. See you tomorrow then.

-Yep, see you tomorrow, I'll be here same time. Bye then.

-Bye.
....

Oh my God, the guy's a conman!, "*Gustavo Losso*" indeed! Well, it will be a while before you're sucking my bones dry, that's for sure.

***

Eight

-"Franci darling, how are you? It's so nice of you to call. No one rings me at the moment.
-Chiara, how are you? I'm fine.
-It's not a great day to be honest. I saw the consultant oncologist yesterday.
-Ah, and?
-It's a big gift! Glioblastoma multiforma. Terminal.
-What, oh my God! Listen, can I come over?
-Not today, may be later in the week.
-Okay.
-She just said: "Look, Chiara, it's not good news, it's terminal". My heart stopped.
-Chiara, I'm so sorry.
-She didn't give me any hope. Nothing. Then I can't remember exactly what she said. My mind went all foggy. Something about the operation being a success and I can start radiation after Easter.
-Listen, I'll call you in a couple of days. And I'll come and see you.

-Yes, that'll be nice
-As soon as you're ready. Bye."

I feel so terrible; I just didn't have the courage to listen her out. My poor Chiara. Women have an incredible capacity for bearing pain, suffering and loss. And they take the pain of the world's suffering upon their shoulders. Our culture is imbued with acts of untold feminine heroism over the centuries. From Joan of Arc to Mother Theresa, and even Lady Diana. And our churches are adorned with statues and paintings of the Virgin Mary's sorrowful eyes to wash away the tears of our desperation. Yes, they want us to love through empathy and compassion. We're meant to love unconditionally - and men opportunistically. And that's how most of us get through life's knocks; we lower our expectations with every blow. And that's why I'll never understand how, despite our cultural imprint of all-enduring devotion, that we women can be so cruel to each other in the face of death. We all fear death. Why couldn't she have told Chiara that it was a very serious cancer and that there was a lot of options ahead to fight it? Chiara is very intelligent and she knows what it means to have a glioblastoma, but this was just like issuing her death certificate before her time. Christ, she's a mother, not a fucking statistic. Who are you to play God with her life?

***

Nine

"Hi, Giuseppina, we're all fine thanks, and you…. Yes, I know Elisa and Giorgio had a bit of a fall out. What's that? Elisa is still distraught because Giorgio didn't come to her birthday party?... Well, Giorgio was offended, and she did say that he had bad breath. It wasn't very nice for him. .. .Yes, of course I accept your apologies, but what can we do? They're kids, and they're just growing up. …Well, I suppose we could all go out as families for a pizza together. Yes, I've always wanted Edo to meet Andrei. I'm sure they'd get on well. They support the same, football team, after all … Right, this is what I'll do. I'll have a talk to Giorgio first and make sure it's alright with him. I'll tell him that Andrei wants to talk to him about his future in the football team. That should work. He is going to move up a category next year. He'll appreciate that….. Good. Listen, tell Elisa not to worry. She's such a sweet and sensitive girl…okay, bye then."

***

Ten

-"Franci, it's Benito here.
-I just wanted to call you to thank you for the way you handled the whole fire issue. Everyone is talking about you up in head office. They know that you saved the day with the damage loss assessor.

-Well, I should be thanking you really Benito. It was all your plan.
-So what happened then? Did he take a shine to you?
-Very funny... Let's just say that feminine charm, like male ignorance, can get you a long way in life! But don't worry Mr Macho, "my heart belongs to only you", ever since the days of Bobby Vinton, in fact. Listen Benito, have you found out any more about the grass who snitched and gave the video to the local newspaper?
-No, but I did get the dirt on Raffaele!
-No way, what's all that about?
-Well, he's been having a secret liaison with Angelica, the hotel housekeeper. We've got video footage of them getting rather steamy in the dirty laundry room.
-No Benito, that's incredible! I've always thought they were up to something. But why didn't I get to know about directly from security? They're supposed to report back to me. Well, I'm going to have to put a stop to it. You know I don't allow any type of fraternisation in my department.
-Franci, that's precisely why your security guards didn't tell you. They didn't want you going on a moral crusade. We have to be very careful about mobbing these days.
-Well, that's true. Okay I'll keep quiet about it for now. But I definitely want to see the video footage.
-Are you asking me to peddle company porn?
-Come off it Benito. I bet you've shown it to all your mates.
-The last thing I wanted to say is more serious. The board didn't take to Conrad's version of events though, and it's

rumoured they're going to move him to manage our Sicilian operations. And he's only got a year to retirement.
-Out of the frying pan and into the throes of Charybdis and Scylla. That must be a real dilemma for him. I wouldn't like to be in his shoes. What do you think he'll do?
-I reckon he'll retire.
-I can't see him wanting to retire yet.

***

Eleven

-"Ciao Franci, come in.
-Chiara you look much better. And you've lost weight too. Oops …. Can I say that?
-Yes sure, at the moment I'm really proud of myself. I'm following a totally vegan diet, and no carbs or sugar of any type. So that's no chocolate or beers either. I've lost three kilos out of choice.
-Chiara, every day you surprise me. How do you do it?
-Well, the way I see it, while I'm in with a fighting chance, I'm going to give it everything I've got. I owe it to myself, my children and Paolo. I'm going to do the radiotherapy and the chemo, and I'm going to get better and be with them as long as I can. If that little "gift" needs to feed on sugar to grow, then I'm going to make him a Dachau victim. Franci, did you know that Nazi's didn't invent concentration camps? It was a Majorcan. You should

definitely think twice before going there for a holiday! His name was Valeriano Weyler y Nicolau, and he was Governor-General of Cuba and the Philippines. He coined the term when he set up "reconcentration camps" in Cuba, while the Americans used them to herd up a whole lot of Native Americans, and the British were trying their hand at it in the Second Boer War, but history seems to have conveniently forgotten them. Being the victors or the vanquished makes all the difference when you're writing history books.

-Chiara, what books have you been spinning out on lately? Are you sure they're good for you right now?

-There's nothing like truth and honesty for a good clean out.

-You're my wounded soldier, but you're such a fighter.

-Well, we'll see. Now Franci, promise me that you'll relax and be yourself, cos' I don't need any of your prep talking. It's our afternoon together. I've really wanted to see your for the last two days… I'm starting to feel back to my old self. What do you want to drink? I'm going to choose from my fantastic selection of two hundred and fifty varieties of green tea. They're all organic but I can't promise that child slavery was not used during the leaf-gathering process at the plantations. Now I could die for that Houjicha leaf, it's really woody! *"Konnichiwa, plincess Flancesca, may I leccomend you the Matcha blend. They serve it at your Matka restaulant, but I do not know how to desclibe the fravour"*- ah yes, that's it …*vely fishy!!*

-*How about a splitz then Plincess Kagami? Have you got any Aperlol?*

-Now that's more like it Franny. So have you aired your fanny lately, or is the dust still piling up? I was thinking of getting you a deluxe vibrating Swiffer kit for your birthday.

-No, of course not. Anyway how are your scars healing Elsa Lancaster?

-Help me out there.... Who's that Franci?

-She was Lily of course, in Frankenstein's Bride... don't you remember her? She had conical hair and white lightning streaks along the sides...

-Look, this is my porthole. Or should I say a window of opportunity?

-Oh, your hair is starting to grow back already. Not as bad as I thought, actually.

-The surgeons were pretty considerate because they left my hair long on top so I can cover it over.

-Hey Chiara, did you know that Mary Shelley, turned to women after her husband's death? The gay revisionists have been talking about it a lot lately.

-Well, all those exiled Italophile Romantic poets were a funny crowd: Byron, Keats and Percy Bysshe Shelley.. they were all a bit homoerotic if you ask me. I wonder what drove her to write Frankenstein, was it her obsession with the Byronic hero, or the sight of her husband in bed with Lord Byron himself?

-And what drove her to pussy, more importantly?

-Guess we'll never know, Franci! Here's to my woody tea, and are you ready to do the *splitz*, my sweet ballerina girl? Cheers!

-Here's to you!

....

-Chiara, you'll never guess what happened to me last week….I decided to learn Transcendental Meditation, thinking it might come in handy sometime.
-Here we go again, a woman with a mission. I can just imagine what you were thinking about, but go on…
-So I met the venerable guru, Gustavo Losso.
-What?
-Yep, that's what he called himself, and he gave me this personalised secret mantra to recite?
-What? You're joking… It wasn't Kyring or something like that by any chance?
-Yes, how do you know? That's incredible!
-You tell your story, then I'll tell mine.
-Well it all went really well until he asked me to for the fee. "It's nine sixty" he said, and I said, "well I've got a twenty euro note. Have you got any change?"
-No way, that's fucking funny!
-Then he said there had been a misunderstanding and he had meant nine hundred and sixty euros.
-Well, I got that. How could you misunderstand him? I'm supposed to be the one with a brain problem. You didn't pay him did you? He's a fraudster. He used to go by the name of Felice Mastronzo. He got arrested a few years ago, but he's obviously back doing the rounds again…and he's still selling one of the most expensive "keyrings" on the market.
-So how do you know all this?

-Well, it's a long story and it all happened a long time ago. You know my mother died when I was very young, not even seventeen. After that, I got into a lot of crazy things: I got into religion, spirituality, yoga, and meditation. You name it and I did it...All in the desperate hope of finding some answers, and place to feel safe; and I wanted a sign from my mother so badly. All I got was abuse: a priest molested me, that guy ripped me off, and eventually I got myself into a real mess with drugs. The social services helped me into a rehab clinic and that's where I spent a couple of years. It was a very hard time, but we all were straight talkers. Nobody faked. One of the hardest things was actually admitting to myself that my pain didn't come from my mother's death. It was already there, and then I had to accept that I was starting to feel better. There was an unwritten code there that you just didn't acknowledge to the other rehabbers that you were going to be fine. You didn't want to make them feel uneasy by your feeling better. But that's where I rebuilt myself and got over my addiction. I learnt to look my pain straight in the eye, and accept it. No running away. And it's very helpful right now. Our pains never go away. They can flame up at any time. But you can accept them. That's how you live with them and take some distance.

-And there's me thinking that I could learn this great technique to help you meditate and de-stress as if it were a detox diet.

-Well, Franci that's very kind, and I appreciate it, really I do, but you're forgetting one very important thing.

-What's that Chiara?

-You're the one that needs to meet yourself, not me.
Well, all I …

-Come on Franci, don't fool yourself. You're wasting your time with me. Have you ever stopped to ask yourself what it is you've been looking for in all these years of holistic foraging? Well let me tell you…. You're looking for that space too, a dimension where you can feel safe and be yourself. And the truth is it's always been there, inside, and you've been there many times. But then you drop it all and throw it away, so that you can go back to the beginning and start again. That's because of distraction. And you know, it really is as easy as sitting by the lake and watching the sunset, or allowing your eye to trace the hypnotic flight of a butterfly moving from one flower to another. This is what you call finding your "inner child"; and when you do, it looks you straight back in the eye and asks you in all candour: are you happy with yourself? with your life? your marriage? your job? And what if your answer is no? You're all alone in your silent space – What do you do? It requires change, action, yes, action now. And so you say, "I know I'll choose distraction, that's easier than change". Change is awkward, you can't know it, it's unpredictable, it's an unharnessed ocean crashing waves upon your heart; it's a ferocious wind whistling round your ears; it's the sodden earth weighing heavily upon your body; and it's a blazing fire raging through the forest of your mind….But if you don't stand your ground and face its torments, you will spend your life on the run, hiding from your miserable existence. So what was that transcendental Yogi's name again?

-Maharishi

-Ah yes, that's the one, and what did he say about prayer, again? I can't quite remember…

-It was something like "no prayer will go in vain. You have to knock and the door will be opened", I think.

-And doesn't that remind you of anything, Franci? A recent sermon, a gospel, perhaps?

-The Gospel of Saint Matthew, yes, you're right.

-Yes, well they all say the same thing, but it's nonsense. Because you can't ask from the bottom of your heart when someone has already signed your death certificate. My prayers can never be answered. I'm a mother and my only option is to pray for remission for as long as possible. And that's why I'm an atheist Franci, and I'm scared. No mother can live peacefully with the knowledge of her impending death, and that she'll never live to see her children grow to be adults. I just want this life; not your heaven, or a thousand lives on the way to Nirvana. Nature gave me ovaries and a lifetime's supply of eggs – one or two million I think, only I'm not sure 'cos I'm still counting – and they've got all the genetic information they need inside to ensure my survival into the next generation. And what my children will remember of me, they'll carry in their hearts. All I want is to be with them from the bottom of mine. And I can't. Darwin died nearly 140 years ago, yet most of western civilisation persists with biblical myths to negate his theory of evolution. I think the flat-earthers are more sane myself.

My best advice is don't make this life a failure under the illusion that you can have another go at it next time round. There is no next time round, or square, or any other shape to stick into the hole, whether it's on heaven or earth, or anywhere you'd care to go in the entire universe. All the religions of the world began because we all fear death, but that should be your excuse for not living your life. Franci, are you with me?
-Chiara I'm listening.
-My god, do you still do that? You amaze me Sister Sledge. We are still family!
-I know you're right, and you're like this because you think you haven't got much time left.
-Franci, can you hug me?
-Come here.

***

Twelve

It's funny to think that just over a month ago, I was obsessed with calculating how long I had to work till retirement.. every day a burden, routine, flat; there I was just going through the motions of life. Not having been particularly ambitious, I was a fairly fortunate Mr Average... and definitely a creature of habit like the vast majority of men I know. My father was a doctor too, a gastroenterologist, and my mother a housewife. I could have lived at home if I hadn't met Franci. We were comfortable, and mum was happy to do everything for me. And to be honest, it wasn't a bad life. The ones that break out of their cast are generally the divorcees or widowers. It's the shock to their system that wakes them up…. But, look at me now, I wonder if my sweet-scented *flower* has been my reawakening; here I am with a spring in my step, out of bed at 6.00am for my early morning jog. I've lost nearly five kilos in a month. Nothing short of a budding Adonis, I'd say. I'm definitely firming up and I'll be in great shape for next weekend, that's for sure. That reminds me, I must call Fiore about plans for the trip.

-*"Lemon tea"…can you call me asap? Storminateacup!"*

….

-"Hi Ed.
-That was quick
-You know me, when there's a buzz in the air…
-Listen, I was thinking that after Friday's dinner and night in Ancona, we could head for the Conero first thing on Saturday morning. There's a hotel I know in Sirolo. Would you like me to plan the trip in detail or play it by ear?
-The latter of course. I'm sure we'll find plenty to do."

***

Thirteen

It's funny to think that just over a month ago my major obsessions were getting my nails polished, colouring my grey hair roots, doing Giorgio's school runs and stressing out about the managing the company fire incident. Now, with Chiara's illness, all these everyday dramas seem like nothing more than an insignificant smudge-cloud squatting momentarily over the setting sun; now he sinks inexorably beyond the skyline abandoning the furrowed sea's tormented brow. Yet that horizon gives me perspective, and tomorrow the sun will rise again for a new day awaits. It's less than a week to our annual conference, and I'm torn between my heart's desire to dip into the porphyry font and bathe my crimson petal, and my moralist catholic upbringing reining in the Mares of Diomedes. I still haven't called Beato, but I know I can't stay out of temptation's way - or his arms - much longer. I'll just drop him a word to let him know I'll be in Rome for the weekend. If I'm lucky, he'll be away, and that will solve the moral dilemma for me. But before that, I've got a couple of old scores to settle.

....

-"Raffaele have you got a minute please? I'd like to comment the new kitchen cleaning procedures manual together before we finalise the text. ...You're just finishing a mail? That's fine.. How about in fifteen minutes? ...Okay. Sure."

…….

-"Well Raffaele, I really think you've done a good job here. Thanks very much again. I think we can we can circulate it next week and then we'll organise a training course.
-If that's everything, then I'll get straight on with inserting the amendments.
-Fine. …Oh Raffaele, there is just one thing actually.
-Yes, Francesca?
-Have you thought any more about your transfer to Maintenance?
-Not really, I'm happy where I am to be honest.
-Well, let me put it another way. We have video footage of you engaging in amorous activities with the housekeeper, Angelica Pompa, in the hotel laundry room.
-Sorry, what did you say?
-Article 5.3 of our Code of Professional Conduct sets out the rules governing personal and romantic relationships in the workplace, and sexual advances are strictly forbidden, and considered a potential cause for dismissal as a distraction from your duties. The Gandalf Group takes a very severe position on female harassment. So what I'm saying is either you agree to the transfer or you are out of the company. What's your choice?
-How long do I have to think it over?
-Zero minutes.
-Okay, I agree to the transfer.
-That's good, I knew you would see reason. Sign here…..

-Your transfer will start on Monday after the Annual Conference. I'll speak with Mutton about it, and we'll arrange a transition period so you can continue to teach the new procedures. Thank you Raffaele. That will be all.

***

Fourteen

It's funny to think that just over a month ago I was planning our annual holiday to Kenya and Tanzania, a beach hut holiday in Malindi, a week's safari to the Serengeti National Park, and trekking on Mount Kilimanjaro with Paolo and the kids. And now I'm staring at a blank wall, imagining my epitaph and consoling myself about the dreams I'll never live. You know, I just don't get this one. I do know some terrible family secrets about my grandfather's abuse of my mother as a child; then there was my uncle's incestuous relationship with his mother-in-law, but they were such a long time ago, and I had to grow up with them. Wasn't it bad enough that I lost my mother at sixteen? And of course, there's Paolo's illicit soirées with the WAGS, but that's our second income. And I silently bought into that too. I've got no one to blame but myself. But I don't blame myself for any of it. I made my choices and I accepted that life's a bitch and just kept looking forward. That was until the visit with my gift consultant. Do I really have to pay such a high price for my childhood drug abuse? I've feel like I've let everyone down, really I do. I'm not even going to do the "why me?" question. I've been there so many times before. I can already picture my funeral. I'm definitely going to get at least another eighteen months out of this life. I'm not just another medical statistics yet.

***

Fifteen

-"Good morning Benito. I'm just a few minutes late. Giorgio missed his alarm call this morning. Spring is always a strange time for sleeping, and his sleep patterns are no exception to the rules. How are you? Have I got some good news for you!
-Well, Franci, I wish I could say the same, but I've got some bad news for you!
-Okay, you start.
-No Franci, I insist.
-Well, the good news is that I got Raffaele to agree to the transfer and he signed.
-No, never! How did you do that?
-Well let's say that he came round to my way of thinking. There's lots for him to do in the Maintenance Department after all. And I can't stand the sight of him any longer.
-Did you threaten him with the video footage?

-I did happen to let slip that there was some compromising video of him washing his dirty socks in the laundry room, yes..

-You're completely mad. Would you like my job here in HR?

-No way Benito, yours is a woman's job. I'd be bored after five minutes.

-Very funny. Are you ready for the bad news?

-Go on then.

-Well, it's about your security guard, Cosimo. We caught him red-handed stealing a leg of ham from the hotel kitchen fridge. Things had been going missing for over a month if you remember, and we'd noticed him loading his oversized sports bag into his car as was leaving the premises; we asked his deputy about his gym training routine, and we discovered he always worked out at 6.00am before he came to work, so it started to seem rather suspicious. We checked CCTV footage and found he usually checked the kitchens late afternoon. He'd told the head chef that he liked to get changed in their locker rooms before he left the company so he could go jogging. I got Conrad to allow me to install a hidden camera by the fridge door, and that's how we caught him.

-And you didn't tell me?

-Well, no, first Conrad didn't want to bother you because we knew what was happening with your friend Chiara, and after all, this was Cosimo, your gay protégé – your bumhole engineer as we call him – who you desperately wanted me to hire as the security guard who was going to make the difference, remember?

-Well he definitely made the difference, so now it's you who wants my job, is it? But just to put the record straight in the global gossip guild of ours, I definitely don't have any friends or favourites here, so make sure you tell me everything next time, or I'll be shopping you for professional malpractice.
-Hey Franci, come off it. This is one step forward, two steps back again. Haven't we done this scene before? You know, I've been thinking that perhaps we should considering doing tango classes together.
-Okay, listen I'll come to your office as soon as I arrive, and we'll discuss the details.
-Tonight, we really must go for an aperitif together. Last time it all fell through.

***

Sixteen

"Francesca, I'm coming to work in the Veneto Region this Friday, and I'll be here for a few days. Could I take you to lunch this time? Call or text me. Beato."

Life always give you what you ask for indeed. There's me sitting on the fence again, hoping that life will hand me all the solutions on a plate without taking any responsibility for it. So, there you are Francesca Scarpa, you've gone and blown it again.

"Beato, irony of destinies. I'm leaving for Rome on Friday morning with the motley crew. It's the Annual Conference and Gala Dinner at the Enchanted Palace on Friday night. Would love to have seen you. So sorry! Franci."

***

Seventeen

-"Chiara darling, how are you? We're having another one of those crazy weeks here.
-Franci, I'm okay, but I've still got another two weeks to go with my radiotherapy and I'm already experiencing tiredness, and nausea. My skin is going dry and itchy too. It's all very localised but it's frightening, really it is.
-Is your hair falling out?
-No Franci, I don't really have any there, my scalp's just really itchy.
-How's your appetite?
-Well that's okay. I 'm still not doing sugar at all. And I don't miss it, But I've not got enough energy to be creative in the kitchen, and the kids are complaining a bit. You need to be a gourmet chef to make half of these vegan recipes.
-Listen, I'll find you a good book, how about that?
-Thanks Franci, you're an angel..why did you call anyway?
-It's nothing really, I'll tell you another time.
-No please, go one, I don't get to hear any gossip these days.

-Well the first reason is that I'm not going to see Beato in Rome this weekend because he's coming here for business.

-That's a major fuck up in my book, Franci. You're usually so good at planning things.

-Yeh, I know, but I went a bit cold turkey on this one, and missed my chance.

-So have you got a plan B to limit the collateral damage?

-Definitely not. You know me.

-Well get one then. This is your first free weekend since last year. You can ring an agency.

-Chiara, no!

-It was worth a try. You must have had one hell of a mother. Was she so strict with you?

-More than you could ever imagine.

-Hmmmm, so what was your other news?

-Well, it was about Cosimo, our wonderful gay head of security.

-What the one you chose specially, Mr Mission Impossible!

-Yes, he got caught stealing a leg of *San Daniele* ham from the hotel kitchen.

-Well, I hope he didn't stuff it down his pants, he would have had a hard time walking to the car.

-No, he stuffed it in his sports bag with his sweaty undies!

-Well, I can think of better ways of curing ham myself, but I wouldn't rule it out as a new flavour option. So when is F&B doing the palate testing? And you want me to be the chief taster, right?

-Benito had a hidden camera installed over the fridge door, and he didn't even tell me. This shit company of ours will never make the grade of a multinational. It claims to be a global group, but it can't even unlatch the door to get out of its own backyard.
-Welcome to the real world, Miss Trinity. Morpheus is next door and he'd like to speak with you!
-Angelo, our hairdresser always said we should keep an eye on him. He'd seen him in action in the clubs, and apparently he had a reputation as a nice bit of rent when was younger. Hey Franci, now he's out of a job, you could consider taking him to Rome to keep your bed warm.

***

Eighteen

-"Benito, that's so nice of you to offer. I'll have a *Campari Spritz* tonight. I need something stronger than usual. A bit of red passion should do the trick. There's not much else going on in my life.
-Hey Franci, it's not the "cougar phenomenon" is it? Because, if it is I've got some good syrup to cure you with.
-What? Are you hinting at Anne Bancroft in The Graduate? You're not a film buff too, are you? I thought you were just a typical Cinderella Man myself. Anyway,

you can keep your cough medicine, thank you. I'll stay with the spritz for now.
-I know we like a joke, but I've always loved the cinema ever since my mum took me to see Cleopatra.
-You continue to amaze me Benito!
-What because you didn't think my brain could stretch to much more than Mad Max, right?
-No, because you're so fucking old! Cleaopatra was 1963.
-You win, Franci…
-No seriously, I'm crazy about films too. Chiara and I have always lived through the Hollywood haze…
-Lived life or abdicated from it? How is she, by the way?
-It's not a great moment, but she's coping. I'm not though. And the worst thing is that she knows it, and she mirrors it back at me all the time. It's her illness, but my epiphany.
-Listen Franci, I wanted to say how sorry I am about our argument over Mutton. I never meant to infer that you had an affair in your past job. It was below the belt, and there's no justification even if I got carried away in the heat of the moment.
-That's okay Benito, it's all in the past now. It was true anyway. I'm sorry too about slamming you for missing your father's death while you were being a skirt-chaser.
-It's not true you know. When my father died, I was on my way to the hospital with my mother, but we didn't make it in time. We'd been home to gather a few personal belongings of hers so she could spend the night in hospital. He'd been a heavy smoker and had to have both his legs amputated over the years due to embolism. He

actually died of an arterial aneurysm. It all happened very quickly. At work, I was a bit of a Latin lover back in those days, and I had just divorced, so I was playing the field so to speak. The rumours grew about me having it away when my father died, and they stuck. Someone had a chip on their shoulder that's for sure. I was careless.
-All the same, I hate malicious gossip.

***

Nineteen

"After carefully considering all the poems submitted for the 2021 edition of the Four Humours Prize for Poetry and Medicine, and as the President of our distinguished jury, I am delighted to announce that we have reached a unanimous decision. Before revealing the winner, however, I would like to thank all participants for their contributions to this year's competition; your works have given us greater insight into the human condition and emboldened our spirits thanks to the love and dedication you demonstrate every day in your work. As truly inspired and creative health professionals, we are proud and honoured to have you all with us tonight. Without you, the world would be a much darker place. Your poetry, like your work, is a gift to all humankind….

Ah, thank you Natasha, as ravishing as ever. Here's the envelope we've all been waiting for….. The winning poem is "The Winds of Change" by Dr. Ed Case. Now, the winner is here, so Mr Case, would you please take the stage to receive your prize, which is a weekend for two in the outstandingly beautiful Sicilian resort of Giardini-Naxos at the Gandalf Beach Resort Hotel. A round of applause for Mr. Case.

....

Now Ed has agreed to recite his poem for us all. So when you're ready, the floor is all yours..

....

-"Renato?
-Ed?
-Fiore?
-Anna?
-Now this is incredible Renato. You're here too! And sorry, who's this you're with?
-Sorry, how bad mannered of me, this is Anna. And Fiore is with you too. They say that in life you always meet twice, and now we meet again ....what a coincidence!
-Anna pleased to meet you.
-You too Ed. Fiore great to see you again. It must be a couple of years now.
-Yes, that's right. How've you been keeping?
-Great. Beautiful place isn't it?
-It is…
....

-So Renato, now I know why you're here. But how did you find out about me and my poem back at the hospital?
-Well, it wasn't hard really. I saw your pseudonym in the list of poems to be published in the anthology and I got a bit curious. Your name wasn't exactly original.
-I guess you're right there. Which was your poem then?
-Ed, it was nothing really. I only wrote it for a joke, interminable nights on the wards.
-Me too. How funny!
-But yours is great Edo. You've a real talent.
-Well if you tell me your pseudonym I'll be very honoured to read yours in the anthology too.
-Okay, but don't laugh. It's Dante Sacripante, and the poem's called Galen's Humours. It's a parody on life using the symbolism of bile – yellow and black, blood and phlegm.
-Right, I'll have a look at that tonight. Are you going on the tour tomorrow?
-No, we're off to Ascoli-Piceno. What about you?
-We're heading for the Conero. A bit of sun-bathing, I hope.
-I know what you mean. Don't blame you.
-Well Anna, Renato, it's been a pleasure. Have a great evening."

......

-"Fiore, this is turning into a disaster. Renato's sure to tell the whole medical staff at the hospital. I'm doomed.
-No, he won't, believe me.

-He's got the dirt on me. Fiore, really, if Francesca finds out… He's divorced, it doesn't matter to him. And I know him too well.
-Okay, Ed, if you want to live out your life's worst fiction fantasy then go ahead, but you can do it without me.
-No Fiore, sorry, let me come back to my senses.
-Listen, he won't tell anyone. That girl Anna. She's a trans. She goes by the name of Anna Drenalina, and she's not had the operation, so in my book that means Renato is….
-What? I don't get this at all.
-Well, while you were chatting with Renato, Anna and I had a few words too. She's a great girl believe me, and your secret is safe with her ….and Renato!
-So how do you know Anna?
-Ed, there are a lot of things you don't know about me too, but I'm not going to allow anything to spoil this weekend for us. Let's just say we powdered our noses in the same boudoir a few years ago."

***

Twenty

Right, I've got five minutes before I meet my colleagues downstairs. I must admit they've really excelled this year with their warm reception. And the flowers - it's a beautiful spring bouquet. I love the boldness of the protea in the centre, carefully attended to by the bright pink peonies, like ladies in waiting. Then there's that stark contrast between the dark-red chocolatey-coloured cosmos and the candid freesia. Oh, the delicate fragrance of the freesia, they really are my favourite. They represent me perfectly. Well, I'm dressed and ready to go. My dark blue *tubino* dress, - Chiara got her way in the end – it is a little bit Audrey, in Breakfast at Tiffany's, I dare say, but even by my own high standards, I must admit I look pretty damn good at forty-four. And Angelo did a great job with my hair too. He said I looked like Botticelli's *Venere*. I wish! It's a while since I've had my golden locks flowing like this though. Not very practical, but this is a special occasion. Ah, there's a card with the flowers, let's see what it says... Oh that reminds, I've got to text Giorgio. I'll read the card later.

-*"Giorgino, how are you? What is Grandma making for dinner? I'm about to go to my dinner myself, so I'll speak to you first thing tomorrow morning. Text me. Mama loves you."*
-*Mama, Grandma is taking me to the cinema, then we're going out for a cheeseburger. Can't wait. Ciao."*

My mother-in-law is just like her son. That's why I don't like Giorgio going there. Everything I forbid, she allows. This is the third time Giorgio has been to McDonalds in a month. He'll have stomach ache all next week.

………..

"Now, that concludes the financial overview of the company so we can move on to more pleasurable pursuits: the Gandalf Global Talent & Leadership Awards. First off - Sense of Responsibility and Duty….

It is with great pleasure that I announce that this year's winner of the Sense of Responsibility and Duty Award is Francesca Scarpa. Francesca is Head of Health and Safety at our regional headquarters in the North of Italy, and many of you know her already. She has been awarded this prize on account of her devotion to the company ideals and her unremitting resolve in dealing with a very delicate incident that could have damaged our reputation and comprised our whole season. In fact, Francesca acted with unprecedented speed and demonstrated consummate organizational skills to ensure that the Enchanted Garden Hotel gourmet restaurant could reopen just two weeks after a fire had completely destroyed the kitchen. More incredibly, Francesca has been doing two jobs for the past month while her colleague recovers from illness. I sure you all agree she is a worthy winner, in addition to being a stunningly attractive lady. Congratulations Francesca…"

…….

Well, that's over and done with. Quite a nice surprise to pick up a prize, admittedly. It's turning out not to be such a bad weekend after all.

Twenty-one

That's so incredible, I haven't slept like that in a long time. I never expected too either. Saturday morning in Rome, I'm not looking forward to the edutainment training day with my colleagues. I'll stick close to Benito; his jokes will jolly me along. Or perhaps I should just bunk off and go on a shopping spree starting out from Piazza di Spagna. Bulgari, Armani, Versace, Hermes and Tiffany are all within close range. I'll think about that one under the shower ..anyway I bagged the prize, so I might as well have some fun now! Ah, there's the card I forgot to read.

"Dear Franci, I had second thoughts… My work can wait. How about breakfast in the Caffè Greco on Saturday morning? Don't text or phone me, I'll be there at 8.30 waiting for you to break my heart! Beato"

Okay, it's five to eight…still not dressed, but this appointment is not about to pass me by.

***

Twenty-two

-"Ah, welcome back to the *Conchiglia Verde*, Doctor Cassese. It's been a few years, hasn't it?
-Indeed it has, Alba, but your hotel hasn't changed at all; still so colourful and welcoming. I hope you're going to serve your wonderful fish broth for dinner tonight.
-I remembered that's what you like, so of course, the cook is already working away in the kitchen - that's five kilos of fish and seafood for the two of you. I hope you're hungry. Well, you've plenty of time to work up a good appetite. All the fish are from this morning's catch: rockfish, monkfish, mackerel and red mullet; then there's the sea food: mantis shrimps, mussels and clams and baby cuttlefish. And I remembered that you don't like green peppers, right?
-Spot on Alba.
-And this is my … ermm…colleague….Fiore.
-It's a pleasure, you'll love it here. Dr. Cassese has been many times. He's one of my favourite clients."

……

-"Stormtrooper, her eyes were nearly popping out of her head when she saw me.
-I know, it was cracking me up too. She looked like a goggle-eyed *matrioska*, whose next of kin was about to pop out from inside her!

-She's definitely got a few stories to tell, and she holds many more secrets.

-Everyone knows her around here. She's been a widow as long as I've known her. She lost her husband at sea, she said before the age of thirty. She never remarried or had children.

-With the way she looked at us, I have no doubt that we are all her children. Listen Ed, it's a beautiful afternoon. Shall we go for a walk along the beach below the cliffs before dinner?

-First things first.

-Come on, you're insatiable."

....

-"Ed, I'm so bloated, I can't manage even the thought of another spoon of fish broth.

-It was so delicious, though. I've got to unfasten my pants – a whole month of dieting gone up in smoke with a fish broth. I'm even coming out in a cold sweat, look at my forehead.

-Oh, Dr. Cassese, you've disappointed me again. You've only just managed half of it. Did we do something that was not to your liking?

--Alba absolutely not. It was incredible. But the portions…. My God, you could have served a whole army with that. We're just gorged, but thank you so much, and please give our compliments to the chef.

-How about coffee?

-Yes, of course two espressos.

-Could you put a drop of grappa in mine?

-Me too, it will help with the digestion.
-We'll have to walk this one off a bit. Let's go up into town.
-You're right Fiore.
-Oh good, I'll tell you my rose story on the way. It's called "The Rose Bud and the Honey Bee".
-Can't wait!

***

Twenty-three

The Honey Bee and the Rose Bud

"Once upon a time, there was a honey bee called Humphrey; in fact, he was a very proud and very hard-working forager bee, and he loved to collect pollen as he buzzed from flower to flower. As a young bee, he learnt the tricks of his trade, following the most expert pollen gatherer, astutely observing his master's techniques. He quickly discerned which flowers would give him most pollen, which were too young, and which were too old. He also became highly skilled at packing pollen into his sacks, and very soon he became the best forager bee in the whole hive. But he was also a generous bee, and was very popular among his bee community, as he would always advise his fellow bees where to gather the best pollen. And he was a very intelligent bee too; he knew exactly when it was time to leave a flower to rest so that she too could enjoy the beauty of nature unfolding before her.

But as time passed, Humphrey grew weary. He knew he would never be close to the queen bee, as it was not his destiny. His role was simply to gather pollen and hand it over to the worker bees who packed it into the hive cells as tightly as possible to make the best ambrosia in the entire vale.

So, one beautiful spring morning in the month of May, he woke early and decided to venture beyond his territory passing through the neighbouring woods, crossing the stream on to the other side of the valley, until he came upon the most magnificent rose bush he'd ever seen. And before he knew it, Humphrey was transfixed by a rose bud of the most exquisite proportions. At first they exchanged furtive glances, then Humphrey grew bold and looped-the-loop soaring on high above Gemma's spinning head until she became quite dizzy. She responded by peeling back one of her sepals to reveal her outermost crimson petal.

That night Humphrey promised he would return. By now he was intoxicated. His fellow foragers warned him not stray into the woods for there were many unknown dangers hidden in the undergrowth, and hornets were nesting in the valley below. But they could do little to restrain him.

Every day, Humphrey returned and gave his adorned rose bud a dew drop, which he deposited on her tip in the hope one day that she would drink with him. They grew fonder and fonder of one another and whispered sweet-scented nothings on the fresh spring air. Then one fine morning, as Humphrey was rounding the final blades of grass in the field before him, he suddenly beheld a daunting sight. Gemma had become a rose in all her splendour. He reddened at the sight of her radiant petals wafting on the gentle breeze; she now held the balance of eternal union between heaven and earth. She was quite simply a paragon of perfection.

In one fell swoop, he dived among the copious folds of her bunching petals and buried himself in her bosom. She peppered him with pollen and showered him with nectar as he caressed her alluring anthers. They were so happy together, and it seemed as if time stood still. Before nightfall, she sent him on his way with the most wholesome bundle of pollen that had ever been gathered. Their loving intensified as the days grew longer and her fragrance sweeter.

Then one morning, the air grew moist and heavy, and Humphrey toiled to fly beyond the woods; clouds were gathering on the horizon. The heavens tarnished, casting a sullen yellow light upon their idyllium. A goldfinch hastily flew down from her nest to warn Humphrey to take refuge in the woods, but he stood firm. He could no longer bear to leave her side.

Then, the heavens opened and the rain began to pelt. The first drop stunned Humphrey and he tailed precipitously towards the earth where he crashed rather clumsily. She beckoned him to rise again so he could nestle in her bosom, but now it was hailing, and he was flattened by the barrage of icy stones. Gemma cast her battered petals down to the ground in desperate hope that she could shelter him from nature's wrath. Alas, no sooner had she shed her last petal upon his injured brow, when a thrush flew down from the trees and snapped him up. The storm passed, and the birds began to sing again. The next day, the rose bush would fill the air with its delicate fragrance and the bees would be foraging for food once more."

***

Twenty-four

-"Hello Stewart. How have you been? You look much better, just like your old self again. I'm so glad you're back now, really I am. It's been an exhausting few weeks.
-Francesca, I don't know how I can thank you enough. Everyone has said how marvellous you have been, and with my team too. I had to take some time off to work through some difficult personal matters. I didn't mean to land you in it, I'm really sorry..
-Stewart, don't apologise. These things happen. And they can happen at any time. We all like to think that we're in control of our destiny but sometimes the painful reality is that we're not.

(Ting!)

"Franci, thanks for an incredible time. I've paused to catch my breath on Saint Angelo's Bridge, I can still smell the sweet fragrance of your hair. Thanks again. Call me when you're free."

-You've never said a truer word, Francesca. Well, I'm back on my feet now. My stomach is still a bit iffy but I think that's the medication I'm on for the time being.

-Ah, well, I hope you'll be able to come off it soon. Did Benito mention that Raffaele had agreed to the internal transfer to your department?

-Yep, and that's fine with me. I could really do with his help in developing our procedures more systematically. They've been neglected for far too long. I was thinking about asking if you'd like a swap with Corrado. He's very good with computers, and Benito thinks you might need someone with good technical skills in that area.

-Well, Stewart, in principle it sounds like a good idea, but let me just check with my team first, and I'll get back to you before the end of the day. Thanks for the offer.

(Ting!)

"Mama, I've got stomach ache in my maths lesson again, Giorgio".

-Sorry Stewart, let me just answer that. It's my son; he's got stomach ache and growing pains. It's always like this on a Monday morning.

-Well, while you're doing that, I'll just pop to the bathroom. Excuse me.

(Ting!)

-This time it's Stewart's phone. He's left it on the table. I wonder who's texting him. I shouldn't peek, but….

"Lemon Tart, just finished in the operating theatre. My head is filled with the sea breeze of Sirolo and your poetic spirit. I feel like a new person. Call me asap. Stormtrooper".

***

ACKNOWLEDGMENTS

A special thanks goes to my MasterChef and dearest husband Fausto, and my parents for their support in my new venture.

Printed in Poland
by Amazon Fulfillment
Poland Sp. z o.o., Wrocław